Fear struck her

D0370623

The office was dest... her.

Ian grabbed her before she could walk in. "Stay here. Let me check it out." He withdrew his gun and slipped past her.

Moments later she followed him inside. Ripped papers and books, smashed objects littered the floor, along with items from storage boxes, a foot deep. She stepped into the bathroom, surprisingly left untouched. Then she saw it. *STOP ME* was written on the mirror in bold black letters. She shook her head, as though in shock, not believing what she was seeing.

"Caitlyn?"

Finally their gazes embraced across the turmoil, tears pooling in her eyes. He came to her and she plastered herself against him, her whole body shaking.

"Why would someone do this?" she asked.

"He left a message on the mirror."

A shudder rippled down her spine. No. "He doesn't want me to stop him. He wants to scare me...and then kill me."

Margaret Daley, an award-winning author of ninety books (five million sold worldwide), has been married for over forty years and is a firm believer in romance and love. When she isn't traveling, she's writing love stories, often with a suspense thread, and corralling her three cats, who think they rule her household. To find out more about Margaret, visit her website at margaretdaley.com.

TEXAS RANGER SHOWDOWN

MARGARET DALEY

⬧ **HARLEQUIN**® LOVE INSPIRED® SUSPENSE

If you purchased this book without a cover you should be aware that this book is stolen property. It was reported as "unsold and destroyed" to the publisher, and neither the author nor the publisher has received any payment for this "stripped book."

LOVE INSPIRED BOOKS

Recycling programs for this product may not exist in your area.

ISBN-13: 978-1-335-49029-2

Texas Ranger Showdown

Copyright © 2018 by Margaret Daley

All rights reserved. Except for use in any review, the reproduction or utilization of this work in whole or in part in any form by any electronic, mechanical or other means, now known or hereafter invented, including xerography, photocopying and recording, or in any information storage or retrieval system, is forbidden without the written permission of the editorial office, Love Inspired Books, 195 Broadway, New York, NY 10007 U.S.A.

This is a work of fiction. Names, characters, places and incidents are either the product of the author's imagination or are used fictitiously, and any resemblance to actual persons, living or dead, business establishments, events or locales is entirely coincidental.

This edition published by arrangement with Love Inspired Books.

® and TM are trademarks of Love Inspired Books, used under license. Trademarks indicated with ® are registered in the United States Patent and Trademark Office, the Canadian Intellectual Property Office and in other countries.

www.Harlequin.com

Printed in U.S.A.

And forgive us our sins; for we also forgive every one
that is indebted to us. And lead us not into temptation;
but deliver us from evil.
–*Luke* 11:4

To the Love Inspired and Love Inspired Suspense editors
Thank you for all your hard work

ONE

Called in by the Longhorn sheriff, Texas Ranger Ian Pierce pulled up to the crime scene outside of town. A woman's body had been found by an older couple out for a morning walk on the country road.

Ian approached Sheriff Tom Mason and shook his hand. He'd been the sheriff in the community when Ian was a teenager. He'd always admired the man and the way he ran his department. The people in this county did too because he'd been in his current position for twenty-five years. "It's good to see you again. I just wish under different circumstances."

"So do I, especially with this one. The woman murdered was Jane Shephard."

"Senator Shephard's daughter?"

Tom nodded. "I figure with a state senator's family involved, I should have you involved too."

"You think it might be politically motivated?"

"No indication of that, but it'll be a volatile case." Tom headed toward the roped-off crime scene. "It appears she was dumped here sometime early this morning. She hasn't been dead long. We'll know more after the autopsy."

Ian ducked under the yellow crime-scene tape and made his way down the steep side of the ditch where the victim lay faceup in about an inch of dirty rainwater, posed with her hands across her chest. No outward sign of how she'd been killed. "Do we know how she died?"

"When we rolled her over, she had multiple stab wounds in her back, but there's little blood on the scene, which rules out this as the place where she was murdered. I'd like to keep the extent of the wounds quiet."

"Any evidence?" Ian asked as he took his cell phone and snapped pictures of the dump site.

"Some smudged footprints in the mud. When Mr. White saw Jane, he thought she might be alive and hurried down the side of the ditch. He slipped once. His actions destroyed some evidence, but I don't know when she would have been found if the Whites hadn't been out for a walk. You can't see the bottom of the ditch from a passing car."

"Have you informed the family yet?"

"Nope. But I'm going over to the house, right after I make sure this is processed correctly and the body's off to the morgue." The sheriff removed his cowboy hat and ran his fingers through his hair. "I've never gotten used to this part of my job."

"I know what you mean. And it would be better coming from you than me. I've only seen Jack Shephard recently on TV. But I can stay here to make sure everything is done by the book, if you want to go now. I wouldn't want him to hear it from someone else."

"I agree. Let's meet later at the station. I'll find out what I can about Jane's whereabouts yesterday and this morning, and especially when her family last saw her and where she would have been going this morning."

"Maybe if we can piece together a timeline of her movements, we can discover where she was murdered."

Tom stuck a toothpick into his mouth and put his hat on his head, then climbed out of the ditch and left.

Three days on the job in Longhorn and Ian had already become involved in the murder of a member from a prominent family. After the intense few months he'd spent in El Paso rounding up a drug cartel, he'd hoped to have a little downtime to deal with his brother and make sure his grandma was all right. Something was wrong with Sean, and he was determined to help his older brother whether he wanted it or not. His grandma was worried sick about Sean. Ian had returned to his hometown because of his family, especially for Nana, who needed more help than she wanted to admit to anyone.

An hour later, the area had been processed, with pictures taken and what little evidence there was collected. Jane Shephard's body had been transported to the morgue for an autopsy.

When Ian left the dump site, he drove toward his grandmother's house. He had promised to have lunch with her next door, at her best friend Sally's, and he was late. He'd forgotten about it until he'd been climbing out of the ditch and had received a call from Nana.

As Ian stopped at a light, his cell phone rang, and he saw it was the sheriff. "How did the family notification go?"

"Jack Shephard wasn't there. He's in Austin. His wife called him, and he's heading back to Longhorn now. Ruth took the news relatively well, but I was glad her housekeeper was with her when I left. Ruth didn't know where Jane was last night, but this morning she left early to meet with her therapist, Caitlyn Rhodes."

Caitlyn Rhodes. Her name brought back good memories but also regret. There were times over the years he could have used her advice and friendship. The closest he'd been to her in years was listening to her radio talk show, where she counseled people who called in. He still didn't understand the abrupt end to their relationship the summer she graduated from high school.

"I'm waiting for Jack to arrive here. He's coming to the station before going home. Can you talk with Caitlyn Rhodes?"

Since he'd returned to his hometown, his grandma had mentioned Caitlyn, who was Sally's granddaughter, several times. "Sure. In fact, I'm supposed to have lunch with her grandmother today. I'll find out Caitlyn's schedule and track her down."

"Do you know her?"

"Yes. We went to school together and were friends, but I haven't seen her in a long time." Too long. Every time he heard her on her radio show he'd pictured her in his mind—petite, long wavy brown hair with a touch of red in it and the most beautiful dark green eyes.

"Call me after you talk with her."

"Will do."

He and Caitlyn had been two years apart in school. She'd been popular and had a lot of guys wanting to date her. While he'd attended a college in Dallas, she'd finished high school and, that summer before she went to the University of Texas, they'd dated several times. He'd begun to think they were growing closer, but suddenly one day he'd received a voice mail from her, canceling their date. Later he discovered she'd left town. Their paths didn't cross after that, and he'd always wondered if they could have had a serious relationship. Now it didn't make any difference. His job was his life.

Caitlyn Rhodes took a moment while several commercials were played on her popular talk show, *Share with Caitlyn*. She'd been on the run the whole morning before coming to the radio station for her live program. Her first therapy client, Jane Shepard, had concerned her at her office earlier today. During her appointment, Jane had paced the room, only sitting down a couple of times. Something was wrong, but Caitlyn couldn't get much out of her. She planned to call her later and see if she would come to Caitlyn's office tomorrow or suggest that she could go to Jane wherever she wanted. Caitlyn couldn't shake her concern.

Melanie Carson, her show's producer, signaled that the last commercial was wrapping up. Caitlyn glanced at the wall clock in the studio. Only five minutes till the end of her show. She had time for one or two more callers.

Caitlyn pressed the button. "Hello. You're on the air."

Silence greeted her.

Seconds passed, so she reached toward the control panel to switch to the next caller when a raspy, deep voice said, "Stop me!"

A chill snaked down Caitlyn's spine. "Stop you from doing what?"

Another eerie quiet filled the dead air. She opened her mouth to say—

Click.

Behind the glass window, Melanie frowned and tapped her watch.

Quickly recovering from the call, Caitlyn leaned toward the microphone and started to say what she did when a viewer got cold feet and shut down on the radio: "Please call me at my office, and we can talk privately." But she couldn't get those words out. They stuck in her throat.

Melanie again indicated her watch to wrap up. Caitlyn pulled herself together and began to speak.

"I can't believe how fast the past hour went, but I'll be back tomorrow, same time, to discuss any problems you need help with. Remember: unresolved problems lead to stress, and stress leads to illness. Keep your mind and body healthy. Call me or write me," she said automatically as she did every show. Then she rattled off her email address for the ones like that last caller who froze when they realized millions were listening to them.

If only I could follow my own advice about unresolved problems.

As she rose to leave the studio, she couldn't shake the coldness that had embedded itself deep in her bones at the two words he'd said.

Stop me!

Not calmly but desperately, as though he was at the end of his patience. That shouldn't have stopped her from saying he could contact her at her office. In her years as a therapist with a doctorate in psychology and counseling, she'd talked with many desperate people.

She headed out into the hallway. What had made her not encourage him to call the office?

The sinister edge to his voice? The sense of urgency?

"Caitlyn, are you okay?"

She stopped and turned toward her producer. "Yes, Melanie. It was clear whoever was on the phone didn't really want help or he would have said more." She'd learned over the years that she couldn't help someone who wasn't open to it. It had been a hard lesson, but it had saved her own sanity with one of her clients in her first year of counseling. She wanted to help people with problems and considered it more than her occupation. But as her grand pappy used to say, you could lead a horse to water, but you couldn't make it drink.

"Good. He was creepy. Probably just a prankster."

Over the past two years, *Share with Caitlyn* had had several pranksters on-air. "Yeah, that's what I think."

"Do you want me to screen your calls before you talk to them?"

She didn't want to put any barriers in place for her callers. So far that had worked for her. Handling those few pranksters hadn't been a big deal. Her listeners knew when the phone was answered it was by her, making their first connection more personal. "No, let's leave it as is," Caitlyn murmured and started for the double doors at the end of the corridor that led to the lobby of the building. And yet as she said that, she still couldn't shake the chill those two words had given her.

"I've got his phone number and, if you want me to, I can block his call from coming through to you," Melanie said from the other end of the hallway.

Caitlyn started to say yes, but she reminded herself that she'd gone into counseling to help as many people as she could—even ones who couldn't pay much. That was why she volunteered at Matthew's Ministries Tuesday mornings. She turned toward her coworker and friend. "No, maybe he wasn't ready to share yet, but he might be later. See you tomorrow, Mel. I have a date with Granny."

"Speaking of a date, the guy I'm seeing has a good friend who would be perfect for you. I'll fix you up, and we all can go out together. Say, next week sometime?"

Caitlyn paused at the exit, shaking her head. "No blind dates. I'm content with my life." Her days were full and she didn't need the added pressure of running the dating gauntlet. Years ago, she'd walked away from that when one man stepped too far over the line and she'd paid for his actions. She shoved the memory away. She refused to let Byron ruin her life any more than he already had. But he somehow managed to creep back into her thoughts at unexpected times.

When she left the station in Longhorn, a small town outside Dallas, she took a deep breath of the warm breeze from the south and relished the rays of the sun hitting her face. Spring. She loved this season above all the others. Glimpsing the clock tower at city hall, she hurried her pace. Granny expected a person to be prompt. She didn't believe in keeping people waiting.

Caitlyn slipped behind the wheel of her restored 1956 red Thunderbird, retracted the top and drove out of the parking lot. She arrived at her grandmother's fifteen minutes later, her shoulder-length hair wind tossed. After running her fingers through her wild strands, she climbed out of her car and strode to the front porch.

Before she could ring the bell, Granny opened the door. "Now I can start lunch."

"You haven't yet?"

"Nope. You were late last week, so I wasn't sure when you would come."

Caitlyn looked at her watch. "I wasn't late last week or today."

Her grandmother entered the kitchen where her closest friend and next-door neighbor, Emma, sat at the table enjoying a cup of coffee. Granny made her way to the refrigerator. "Yes, you were."

"Not by my watch." Caitlyn checked its time against the clock over the stove. "Which is five minutes off yours."

"See? I told you that you were late."

"I've got a client at one," Caitlyn said, remembering how several of her weekly luncheons with Granny were full-course dinners. She thought Caitlyn was too skinny.

"It won't take long. I'm only fixing sandwiches. Emma and I have yoga this afternoon. You should join us sometime." Granny pulled a bowl and mayo from the fridge.

"Caitlyn, we listened to your show today." Emma sipped her drink. "You gave some good advice and did a nice job handling that last caller. I would have hung up after two seconds of silence. You're more tolerant than I am."

Granny harrumphed. "You should be less tolerant. I don't like you doing this talk show, four times a week. No telling who it's exposing you to."

Caitlyn sat across from Emma. "I've been practicing for seven years without any problems. I went into my profession to help people who were having problems. Y'all need to stop worrying about me." She knew from personal experience what happened when you ignored your problems for years, hoping they would go away. They never did.

"That's what a grandma is for—to worry about her grandchildren." Granny brought the plate of sandwiches to the table and set them down, then went back for the pitcher of iced tea.

"I'm giving you the okay not to." Caitlyn grabbed a chicken salad sandwich.

"But what about that creepy-sounding man? 'Stop him' from doing what?"

Granny said a prayer, then poured iced tea in both Caitlyn's and her glasses, while Emma stuck to her coffee. "You don't have to take us to yoga."

"My grandson said he'd give us a ride. He should be here any minute." Emma took a bite of her lunch.

"Sean?" Caitlyn was asking about him because lately he'd been more a recluse than a rancher.

"No, Ian. I can never get Sean to do anything lately."

"Ian? I thought he lived in El Paso." Caitlyn remembered the times she, Sean and Ian used to play together as kids. Granny and Emma had been best friends for over sixty years, so it made sense that she'd be friends with Emma's grandkids. Then later, she'd even gone out with Ian a couple of times after graduating from high school and before her life took a detour and they lost touch.

Emma smiled. "Not since last week. A position opened up. He's been transferred to Company B and will be working in the Longhorn area. I've sure missed him. He's staying with me until he finds a house."

"Not at the family ranch outside town?"

"No, Sean and Ian don't get along."

Caitlyn hadn't seen Ian in years. When he had been in Longhorn for his father's funeral last year, she'd been gone. According to Emma, he was so busy with his job as a Texas Ranger that he'd had limited time to come home. What made Ian return now? A change of scenery? His older brother, who was supposed to be looking after Emma, rarely came by. Was that why, or was there something else?

"That's a shame. They used to be so close when we were growing up. I never see Sean anymore, and we live in the same town."

"That's because you're dedicated to your work like both my grandsons, Caitlyn. Since my son died, Sean's been throwing all his energy into making the Pierce ranch the biggest one in the area. He's carrying on the feud my son and his neighbor, Jack Shephard, had over whose ranch was the biggest and richest. He doesn't have time for much else." Emma drained the last of her coffee and set her mug on the table.

The sadness in Emma's voice told Caitlyn there was more to what was going on with Sean than working too much. From all she'd heard, Sean had changed a lot in the past few years—more bitter and angry. His father's death had sent him in a downward spiral. She hated hearing he was continuing the feud between the ranches. "Let me refill your coffee."

Caitlyn rose and walked to the stove to grab the pot. As she turned to come back to the table, Emma shot Granny a *be quiet* look. Caitlyn would have a word with her grandmother when Emma wasn't here. Something was going on. Maybe Caitlyn could help? Emma was like a second grandmother to her. Growing up, she'd been closer to Ian than she was to Sean.

In fact, she'd hoped there could have been more between her and Ian, but she'd had to leave Longhorn suddenly. A relationship with him was never meant to be. Her job fulfilled her, and she was able to do what she loved—helping others.

* * *

As Ian parked in his grandma's driveway, he noticed a retro Thunderbird with its top down parked at the curb in front of Sally's home. He whistled. Beautiful car. Was that Caitlyn's? The sports car had to be hers. It fit her personality. When he'd known her, she'd been serious but with a touch of mischief. How much had she changed? He certainly had, he reflected.

He rang the bell and, not a half a minute later, Caitlyn Rhodes opened her grandmother's front door. A smile dimpled her cheeks and brightened her green eyes.

"It's great to see you." Caitlyn gave him a quick hug, then stepped to the side. "Come in. The dynamite duo will have someone to interrogate besides me now."

Ian chuckled, taking in how much Caitlyn had changed since he'd last seen her five years ago at Christmas. Her usually long brown hair was cut shorter, which framed her face, emphasizing her attractive features from a pert nose to the longest eyelashes to full lips.

He realized he was staring and looked away, trying to tamp down his racing pulse. "Nana has done her share of drilling me for information long-distance."

Caitlyn shut the door, clasped his arm and started for the kitchen. "You're late. Prepare yourself. Being late in Granny's house is frowned upon."

She used to hook her arm through his in the past. Her touch felt familiar and yet…something much more. If only Caitlyn hadn't left that summer, things would have been different between them.

"I'm glad you're here finally. I have a patient at one, so I can't stay as long as I wish."

"I have unusual hours. Crime doesn't work on a schedule."

She laughed. "Neither does a patient's crisis. I understand."

When they approached the kitchen, he let Caitlyn go ahead of him, her arm slipping away from him. He missed the connection. She had always made him feel better and, after the morning he'd had, he needed that. After lunch, he'd talk to her about Jane.

He paused in the doorway. A place waited for him at the table, food already on his plate. He went to his grandmother, kissed her on the cheek and sat down across from her. Nana and Sally were two people who probably knew more than most what was going on in Longhorn. They had lived here their whole lives and were always involved in the church and town. Maybe they'd know something to help with his latest case. "Sorry I was late. I got delayed with a new case."

Sally waved her hand. "Some things can't be helped. I certainly understand."

Caitlyn's eyes grew wide. "He's half an hour late and you don't care, while I was only five minutes late and I got—"

Nana patted Caitlyn's hand. "Honey, I understand. I'd be late if I had a creepy man call me on-air like you did."

Creepy man? Ian shifted his attention to Caitlyn. "On your radio show?"

"You know I'm on the radio?"

He nodded. "I've even listened."

Color flooded Caitlyn's cheeks. "In El Paso?"

"Yep, we have a station that runs *Share with Caitlyn*. It's always nice to hear a voice from my past." He'd felt connected to his hometown—and her—while listening to her on the radio. He could have used her insight on the woman he'd been engaged to, who'd stolen his identity and money, then disappeared. But Caitlyn hadn't been a therapist at that time. Thankfully, after years of being a law enforcement officer, he wasn't as gullible as he'd been when he was in his midtwenties, but the incident wasn't something he'd shared with anyone. "What did this guy say?"

"'Stop me!'" Emma said before Caitlyn could. "But the worse part was the silence."

"Nana, if I was on the radio, I'd have long silences too." Ian caught Caitlyn's gaze and held it. "I admire how you deal with all the different problems people call about." When he'd been growing up, he'd often come to her for advice, so her career choice hadn't surprised him.

She grinned. "Talking has always come easily to me. But I've had many people freeze up when they go live on the radio. Some I never hear from again. Others get over it and ask me to help them."

"I hope that guy isn't one that calls again." Sally took a drink of her iced tea.

"You said you have a new case. What is it?" Caitlyn asked him.

"Now that the family has been notified, I can tell you. Jane Shephard was found murdered outside of town in a ditch."

His grandma's jaw dropped. "Jack is in Austin. Poor Ruth's all by herself."

"The senator is on his way home."

Nana looked at Sally. "We'll need to go to the church and organize some support for them. Jane was their only child. They will be devastated." She rose and took her plate and mug to the sink.

"Yeah, we can't go to yoga. We need to call the people on the church's phone tree." Sally joined her friend at the counter.

When they headed toward the hallway, Ian asked, "Do you want me to take you to the church later?"

"Yes," Nana said as she and Sally began making plans.

Ian swiveled toward Caitlyn, who stared at a spot on the table between them, color drained from her face. "Jane was younger than me in school, but you were closer in age. Did you know her very well as adults?"

"Yes," she said and lifted her gaze to his. "She's— was one of my patients. When did this happen?"

"Based on her lividity when I saw her, she was probably killed between 8:00 and 10:00 a.m."

"Make that between nine and ten. I had an appointment with her at eight this morning. She left my office a few minutes before nine." Caitlyn shook her head. "I can't believe this."

"What can you tell me about her? Was anyone threatening her? Harassing her?"

Caitlyn stood and gathered up her dishes. "I need to talk to her parents first. I don't think what we talked about had anything to do with her death."

"I need to re-create her steps. Did she mention going anywhere after her session?"

"She was meeting a couple of her Dallas friends for lunch and shopping afterward."

"Who was she meeting?"

"Terri Hudson and Zoe Adams."

"Was she dating anyone?"

"The last serious relationship she had was Max Collins, but that ended months ago. Come to think of it, they got into a big fight at Longhorn Café right before Christmas. Max accused her of seeing someone else."

"Who?"

"Frankly, I'm not sure. She didn't discuss it, so I'm not sure she was dating another guy at the same time." She took the dishes to the sink. "I'd better leave now if I'm going to make my appointment."

"I'll walk you out to your car."

"You don't have to. As far as what she was going to do right after seeing me, I don't know anything more. She was dressed casually, as though she might be going back home until she met her friends for lunch. What was she wearing when you saw her?"

"Jeans, boots and a blue blouse."

"That's what she had on for her appointment." Caitlyn grabbed her purse on the counter. "I can tell you that what she was seeing me for wouldn't have made her a target for a murderer."

"People murder for all kinds of reasons. Any insight into Jane would be welcomed." Ian followed Caitlyn from the kitchen. "Having been away from Longhorn for years makes me realize I don't know the town like I used to. Considering your occupation, I'm thinking you do." A woman had been discovered killed with no obvious reason in a town where murder was very rare. He opened the front door and let Caitlyn go outside first. "If that caller hassles you, please let me know."

"I'll help you any way I can. Just like old times." She strolled beside him down the sidewalk toward her car. "But I won't need your help. For all I know, the caller doesn't even live in Longhorn."

He gestured toward her Thunderbird. "When did you get this baby? I'm jealous."

"Nine months ago, when my program was syndicated across the country. It's my one extravagance. I live in a two-bedroom town house. Nothing fancy."

He put his hand on the door handle and glanced at her. "And I'm sure you're going to let a good friend like me drive it soon."

She laughed. "Not until I see how good a driver you are now. When we were growing up, speed was all you thought about when you got behind the wheel."

"I'm older and wiser now. Plus, I've taken a driving course to teach me the finer points of a high-speed chase."

"And that's supposed to make me feel better?"

Ian smiled as he opened the driver's-side door.

Caitlyn started to slip into her seat but halted halfway, her stare fixed on something in the car.

Ian looked in the same direction.

On the white leather driver's seat lay a photo of Jane in the ditch, dead. Written across the top were the words *Stop me!*

TWO

Caitlyn couldn't take her eyes off the same words she'd heard from the caller.

Stop me!

All the feelings of the morning began to overwhelm her, leaving her shivering despite the sunlight beating down on her shoulders.

A hand touched her arm. She gasped and jerked away, nearly falling on top of the picture of Jane.

Ian gripped her upper arm and kept her upright. "Sorry. I didn't mean to scare you. I wanted you to step away from your car. Besides the photograph, there may be other pieces of evidence left behind."

She scanned the interior of her Thunderbird. "What?"

"Fingerprints. Maybe something else. This is clearly connected to Jane's murder."

Jane's killer had not only called her show but had approached her car and placed the picture on her seat in the past forty-five minutes. Brazen. Another chill shimmied down her body. She would never again leave the top of the car down while not sitting in it. Longhorn had its crime, but generally it was a peaceful town.

"I have a client coming to my office in—" she

checked her watch "—fifteen minutes. I try to always be on time, especially with this patient."

"I'll call the chief and have an officer stand guard while I take you to work. Do you know if any of the neighbors have security cameras that might show your car or the street?"

She shook her head. "However, there are a few older couples who are at home during the day. Someone might have seen the person."

"I hope so." Ian retrieved his cell phone from his pocket and walked a few steps away while talking to the police chief of Longhorn's small force.

Could she be the next victim? Why would the killer call her at the station? Did he take Jane when she left Caitlyn's office this morning? The desperate ring to his words replayed in her mind. Did he genuinely want help to stop him from murdering again or doing something even more sinister? She clasped her hands to keep them from shaking. She wanted to help others, but she didn't have the answer for everyone. She'd found that out the hard way, especially six months ago with a patient, not long after syndication.

"An officer will be here shortly. We need to let our grandmothers know what happened."

"I'll go in and talk to them while you wait."

As she left Ian, she quickly called her practice and told the receptionist she might be a few minutes late and to let Charles Thorne know. She hated not being there on time because Charles was one of her clients who was obsessive-compulsive. He detested change in any form. It would take half his session to calm him down.

Caitlyn entered her grandma's house. "Granny, where are you?"

"In the den."

She hurried toward the back of the house and found both ladies sitting near the desk as Emma hung up the phone. "Ian has to take me to work." She paused, fortifying herself with a composing breath. "Because he needs to process my car for fingerprints."

Before Caitlyn could explain why, Granny's eyes grew huge and she asked, "Whatever for?"

"Someone left a photo on my front seat."

Her grandmother pushed to her feet using the desk and chair to steady herself. "What aren't you telling me?"

"It's a photo of Jane's body."

Emma splayed her hand over her chest. "Oh, my! Why?"

This part she wished she didn't have to tell the ladies, but it would come out eventually and Granny would be mad at her for not sharing it with her right away. "The words *Stop me!* were on the picture."

Her grandmother collapsed onto the chair, her hand going to her mouth. Stunned into silence, she simply stared at Caitlyn.

"What's my grandson doing about it?"

Caitlyn shifted her gaze to Emma. "Everything he can."

"Tell him not to worry about taking us to church. We'll continue to organize help for the Shephards from here."

"Thanks, Emma. I'll let him know." Caitlyn turned to her grandmother, who still hadn't said a word. "Granny, I'll call you later from the office. Don't worry. Ian is on the case." She heard the front door open and the soft sound of footsteps coming down the hall.

Emma took her friend's hand. "And, Sally, he's the best. He'll find the killer."

Finally, Granny straightened her slumped shoulders and stared right at Caitlyn. "Make him stay with you. Protect you."

Ian stopped behind Caitlyn. "Sally, I'll do just that. Caitlyn and I have been friends for a long time. I won't let anything happen to her."

"You'd better not, young man."

Caitlyn could see her grandmother was recovering from the news and was working herself up. "We've got to go." She spun around, grabbed Ian's hand and rushed toward the exit before Granny came after her. She didn't stop until she was sitting in Ian's SUV, while he rounded the hood and hopped into the driver's seat.

"I take it she wasn't too happy with the turn of events." He started the vehicle and pulled out of his grandmother's driveway.

"It's not often Granny is speechless."

Ian whistled. "You should consider staying with your grandmother until the killer is caught."

"I can't do that. It could put her in danger."

"He called you after he killed Jane. Did it sound like he was bragging about murdering her?"

"No, not at all."

"I don't think he's targeting you. I think he wants help. By putting the photo in your car, he's again telling you to stop him."

"Like he's desperate? Or he's taunting me?" She'd fought to put her life back together years ago and had—or so she'd thought. Now a killer wanted her to stop him. How?

"Both are possible." Ian pulled into the parking lot next to the clinic where she worked. "I'll walk you in."

"You don't have."

"Yes, I do. Your grandmother will ask when I return and check your car."

She exited the SUV at the same time he did and met him at the front of his vehicle to head into the building. "When do you think you'll be finished with my car?"

"An hour or so. I don't want to miss anything. When is your last client today?"

"Five."

"I'll come back and pick you up then." He opened the main door for her. "Let me have your car keys."

She stopped just inside the one-story building and cocked an eyebrow. "Why?"

"For me to take a spin around town." He chuckled. "Although I would like to do that, it's really for putting your top up when I'm through processing the car."

She plopped the keys into Ian's hand and turned to go to her office. When he followed, she slanted a look at him. "This place is filled with people. I'll be fine." She nodded at Rob Owens, a male nurse at the clinic, and at Claire Sanders, the office manager, who was coming out of the break room and passed them in the hallway. "See?"

"I'm sure you will be. I want to know where your office is because I'll come here later."

Rounding a corner, she paused and unlocked the private entrance to her office. "Thanks." When she started to close the door, he clasped her arm. The light touch of his hand on her skin produced goose bumps. Her gaze connected with his for a long moment, drinking in the sight of him after so many years—tall, well-built, dark hair cut short and hazel eyes that changed colors with his mood. She hadn't realized how much she'd missed him being in Longhorn. His presence made her feel safe, protected.

He smiled, two dimples appearing in his cheeks. "Stay here until I pick you up."

"I will. If you aren't here when my last patient leaves, I have files I need to update."

He stepped back, staring at the door as if he was going to come into her office instead of leaving. If she was truthful with herself, that brief contact brought forth feelings she'd had the summer after she'd graduated from high school. She'd begun thinking of him as more than just a good friend, but then everything changed for her.

Quickly, she shut the door and locked it. When the phone on her desk buzzed, she hurried across the office to answer the call from the receptionist. "Is Charles Thorne here?"

"Yes, he was running late and came in only a moment ago."

Strange. Charles was never late. "Okay. Send him in." Caitlyn headed for the other door into her office and swung it open as Charles approached, his forehead set in a scowl.

He flung himself onto the couch. "I wish I hadn't gotten out of bed. Nothing is going the way it should today. I kept you waiting. I'm sorry about that. It won't happen again."

"What delayed you?"

"A traffic accident. It blocked the street for ten minutes." Then he went on to mention every small thing that had thrown him off, starting with him getting up late because his alarm clock hadn't gone off. "I always set it. Someone must have come into my room and clicked it off."

"Who might have, Charles? You live alone, right?"

He shrugged. "I never *don't* set it. That's the only explanation that makes sense."

"This world is full of change. As much as you want to control every aspect, you can't all the time. Did you stop and take deep breaths?" The last time she saw Jane leaving her office popped into her mind. Could she have done anything to prevent Jane's murder? What if she could have—

She wrenched her thoughts back to her patient across from her.

"No, I didn't have time. I was already five minutes off schedule. I tried rushing, but that made it worse." He kept looking at his watch as his chest rose and fell rapidly. "And now with the accident, I'm fifteen minutes behind. I feel out of control. I can't deal with this." Red flushed his face.

Up until recently, he'd been able to deal with small changes, thanks to a few techniques she'd helped him incorporate into his routine. What was causing this?

"Dr. Rhodes, you have got to stop me!" He held out an arm, his hand shaking.

Stop me! It was as if an arctic blast of wind swept through her office. She hugged herself to keep the trembling at bay.

Those words again! Had Charles listened to her radio show? Or was it something else?

That evening, Ian escorted Caitlyn to his SUV at her office. "Did anyone from work say anything to you about the caller on your show this morning?" He opened the front passenger door.

"The receptionist. She was on break and one of the nurses was listening to the end of my show. *Creepy* was their description."

"And yours?"

"I'd have to agree with *creepy*. I've worked with people who have problems, a few barely functioning day-to-day, but there was something in the way the caller said those two words that set off alarm bells."

"I've talked with Sheriff Mason, who I'm assisting on this case, and we aren't revealing that you received a photo of the victim with the words *Stop me!* on it. If he's doing this for attention, we don't want to feed into it."

"I agree. The press would have a field day with it. My patients could be affected by the publicity. That's unacceptable."

Ian stopped at a red light and glanced at her, seeing that the events of the day had left their mark on her, based on her slumped shoulders, tired eyes and furrowed forehead. He wished he could have changed the circumstances and the killer had never brought her into the middle of the murder. Why had he? The thought left a hollow sensation in Ian's gut. "How did your afternoon sessions go?"

"Okay. My first client was later than I was, which pushed everybody back twenty minutes. Thankfully, the others after him are patient about waiting. A few of mine aren't."

Ian made a left turn. "I got a call from my brother's housekeeper, Alice. She wanted me to come to the ranch. Sean hasn't come out of his bedroom all day. When she last saw him last night, he'd been drinking. Today when she knocked on his door, he didn't respond. When she tried to turn the knob, it was locked." Sean's and his relationship had grown further apart as the years had passed and totally broke down when their father died last year.

"And you want me to come?"

"Yes, but I'll understand if you want to go to your grandmother's house instead."

"I'll go see Sean. I've been worried about him. He's becoming more reclusive."

"Yeah, especially since Dad died nine months ago. It's one of the reasons I transferred here. He hasn't dealt well with it."

"What are the other reasons?"

"Nana. She's beginning to be forgetful. Sean used to check on her frequently, but now he doesn't. When Mom died, Nana stepped in and helped raise us, while Dad ran the ranch. I was six when she died, and my grandma is really the only mother figure I had." His mother's riding accident had affected him, but not nearly as much as it had Sean, who'd found her in the field behind the house.

"With all that's happened, I'd better call and let Granny know where we're going. She knows about the photo. Have you talked to her about not saying anything about it?"

"Yes, when I went back to process your car. Nana too."

"Good. I don't want them connected in any way with the murder investigation." Caitlyn dug into her purse for her cell phone.

"Speaking of the investigation, we need to consider that one of your patients could be the killer."

She dropped her cell phone onto her lap and twisted

toward him. "Because Jane was seeing me or because you think it's one of my patients?"

"Because the guy has pulled you into this."

"That doesn't mean one of my patients is the murderer."

"It doesn't mean he isn't. I'm concentrating my investigation on Jane. Who would want her dead? Who has she been seeing? But I have to investigate all angles. This afternoon, after talking to your neighbors—who saw no one by your car, by the way—I interviewed people where Jane worked." Other than hearing that Jane was a wonderful, giving woman, who'd dedicated her life to running the Shephard Foundation, he'd come up with little information to help with the case.

"Believe me, I want this person caught as much as you do. I'll go through my list of patients and see if anyone jumps out at me. How about the phone number he used to call me this morning?"

"He used Jane's cell phone."

Caitlyn sucked in a deep breath. "I was hoping the caller wasn't the killer, but I guess that's wishful thinking now."

"Yes, since he left the photo and used her phone."

"And was in front of Granny's house, while I was inside." She folded her arms over her chest.

He sliced a look toward her. "Call your grandma. Let her know we're stopping at the ranch. Don't tell her about the call coming from Jane's phone. She and Nana don't need to worry any more than they already are."

"Neither do I."

While Caitlyn made her call, Ian reviewed what little he'd discovered when he'd talked with Jane's two closest friends. Terri and Zoe said they didn't know where she went after seeing Caitlyn or anything about Jane's whereabouts the day before. They both thought she'd stayed at the Shephard ranch yesterday, not feeling well. They didn't know of her dating anyone seriously after Max and she broke up. Ian and the sheriff had met at the ranch Jane's family owned, next to the Pierce family's land, and gone through it. The only thing out of place was her missing car. He couldn't find anyone who'd seen Jane after she left her therapy appointment.

When Caitlyn finished talking with her grandmother, she shook her head. "I've changed my mind about staying with Granny. She wants me to and said if I didn't, then she was going to come to my town house. With all that's going on, I think we'd be safer next door to you. Did you say anything about me staying at her place?"

"No, I only mentioned it to you earlier." The sight of her reinforced all the reasons he needed to find the killer. As a child, he'd been her protector, and he would be now. The guy had involved Caitlyn. Why? He didn't like any of his answers. "I figured I could talk you into it." He smiled at her.

Her eyebrows shot up. "You did? You're awfully sure of your powers of persuasion."

"Well, if that didn't work, then I was going to let Granny know about that time you broke her favorite lamp."

She shot him a glare. "Traitor! It was an accident. I knew how much she loved that lamp. Gramps gave it to her that year for her birthday. You know, I have a few incidents that I could blackmail you over."

He chuckled. "Yep, and that's the reason I haven't said a word."

"Smart man."

As he turned into the main gate at the family ranch, he slowed the car. After he'd moved back to Longhorn this past weekend, he'd come out to see Sean, but the housekeeper had told him his brother was gone. Today when she'd called, she admitted that Sean had insisted she say that or he would fire her. Alice had been with the family twenty-five years. For Sean to resort to threatening her didn't bode well for this meeting.

They hadn't openly fought, but they had drifted apart with the state of Texas between them. Sean and he were only two years apart but, in many ways, they were strangers, even as they grew up, and especially after their mother died.

Ian parked in front of the large two-story, white brick house with four white columns and switched off the engine. But for a long moment, he just sat there, gripping the steering wheel and trying to decide how to deal with his older brother—if he even saw him.

"Worried?" Caitlyn asked.

"Yes. We once had a good relationship, but over the years it's deteriorated." He explained what happened when he came to see Sean the past Sunday. "We've talked on the phone a couple of times, but when I make the call, it always goes to voice mail."

"Has it been that way since you left?"

He shook his head. "Mostly since Dad's passing last year."

"He could still be grieving."

"I thought about that, but I think it's something else. That's why I'd like you here. If I suggested he see you, he wouldn't. He's like Dad was. He won't admit when he's not doing well—physically or emotionally."

"I'll do what I can." Caitlyn scanned the pastures and buildings. "It looks like he's keeping the ranch up."

"Yes, because the foreman we've had for years does a great job. I didn't have a chance to talk with him on Sunday, but I will soon. He's probably gone for the day. I don't see his truck by the barn." He rarely avoided an issue that needed to be dealt with, and he couldn't avoid Sean any longer. "Let's go."

Before Ian and Caitlyn reached the front door, it opened. Alice, petite with sal-and-pepper hair pulled into a bun, waited in the entrance. A frown carved deep lines into her face.

"Sean's in his room. I heard a crash followed by sounds like stuff being smashed against the wall and floor. When he didn't answer my knock, I tried my master key. He must have a new lock. I couldn't get in. I'm afraid he's hurt."

As Ian headed for the staircase, he asked, "How long has he been in his room today?"

"I heard him come home midmorning. I was in the kitchen and didn't know until I heard a crash from the foyer. He knocked over a table by the staircase." Alice gestured toward an empty place along the wall. "A leg broke as well as the lamp and the bowl on it."

Drunk, no doubt, since he'd been drinking yesterday. "Did you see him then?"

"No, but I heard his door slam shut when I came into the front hall."

On the stairs, Ian pivoted toward the older woman. He didn't want Sean to blame Alice for him being here. He didn't know what to expect from his older brother anymore. "We'll handle this." As they ascended the steps, he grabbed Caitlyn's hand. "I won't take no for an answer. I want you to stay in the hall. If my brother attacks me, call the sheriff." He passed her his cell phone. "Use my recent-calls list."

Ian approached the door and knocked. "Sean, it's Ian. Let me in."

After a full minute, he repeated his request, waited twenty seconds, then put all his power behind a kick right under the lock. Nothing happened. He did it again. On the third attempt, the door flew open.

As he moved into the trashed room, Caitlyn side-stepped until she could look inside, but she didn't go in.

It appeared as though no one was in the bedroom. Ian's heart thumped against his chest, adrenaline pulsing through his body as he scanned the chaos of items smashed into shards on the carpet, all the objects on the tables and dresser swept onto it too. One nightstand had toppled over.

When Ian rounded the king-size bed, he found his brother on the floor, lying on tousled sheets, blood staining the white linen.

THREE

When Ian stiffened next to Sean's rumpled bed, Caitlyn came to the entrance with the phone in her hand. "What's wrong?"

"Call 9-1-1." Ian knelt beside the far side of the bed.

As she punched in the numbers, she hurried into the room. "What happened?"

Ian reached down to check Sean's pulse and breathing. "He's unconscious and has a head wound."

Caitlyn reported the emergency, then returned Ian's phone. "It looks like someone tore this place apart. Do you think he interrupted a robber?"

Ian carefully rolled Sean onto his back, then glanced around. "Check the window to see if it's unlocked."

Caitlyn inspected the locks, then turned back to Ian. "Unless he let them into the room somehow, no one got in here by the window."

He hovered over his brother, removing a sheet tangled around Sean's feet. "Maybe he got up, tripped on something and, when he went down, he hit his head against the corner of the nightstand." He examined the piece of furniture. "There's blood on it." When he shifted his attention to Sean again, he leaned down and sniffed the air. "He reeks of alcohol."

"I've never seen him drinking liquor."

"He hasn't since he crashed his car into a tree when he was a teenager. He broke an arm and a leg. This is new, or he's kept it a secret."

Caitlyn covered the short distance to the trash can and picked up a bottle of whiskey. "Is this what he's been doing up here in his room?"

"Probably, but last night he left the house and came home this morning. I'd say he was drunk then, since Alice said he knocked over the table in the foyer."

Sean groaned and tried to curl onto his side.

Ian stopped him. "Sean?"

His brother moaned, resisting Ian's attempt to keep him faceup. "What in the—" He struck out at Ian.

"Sean, it's me. Ian."

Sean blinked his eyes open. "Leave me alone."

"That's not going to happen."

Sean's gaze fixed on Caitlyn. "What's *she* doing here?"

"I'm here to help," she answered.

"I'm fine."

Caitlyn moved closer, half expecting him to leap to his feet and demand she leave, but she would stay if Ian needed her. He'd been there for her earlier. She would be there for him now. "I'm not leaving until the paramedics check you out. You have a nasty bump on your left temple, and it's still bleeding."

Sean tried to lift himself up on his elbow, but instead, he closed his eyes and fell back, wincing. "Leave me alone. I don't need any help."

"Well, you're going to get it whether you need it or

not." Ian rose. "I'll get something to stem the blood flow."

Caitlyn squatted down where Ian had been. "You may have a concussion. If so, you need to have it looked at. Are you dizzy?"

"No," Sean said, his eyes still shut.

"Does your head hurt?" Blood oozed from a gash on his temple, and she leaned closer to examine the injury.

"No. I. Am. Fine." Sean's dark eyes popped open, his pupils enlarged. "Leave. Now."

The anger she glimpsed in his eyes wasn't directed at her but at Ian, who had returned and was standing behind her. With gauze in hand, he knelt again beside his brother.

"We aren't leaving." His jaw set in a firm line, Ian hovered over his brother and stared at him, a silent battle of wills playing out. "I'm going to wrap your head to stop the bleeding. You aren't running me off like before. This is my home too, you know."

Sean glared at Ian but let him tend to his cut.

The chimes of the doorbell echoed through the house.

"I'm not going to the hospital." Sean narrowed his eyes on Ian. "You know how I feel about hospitals."

"You lost consciousness. That's serious." Caitlyn rose to make room for the paramedics she heard coming down the hall.

"I passed out from drinking. Not the same thing." Sean gripped the wooden bed frame and started to hoist himself up.

Ian grasped Sean's arm to aid him.

"Get out. Paramedics can patch me up." Pain mingled with Sean's anger, causing the creases on his face to deepen.

When Alice escorted the two EMTs into the bedroom, Caitlyn stepped back and moved toward her by the doorway.

The housekeeper shook her head. "I don't understand what's been going on for the past few months."

Caitlyn drew Alice into the hallway. "What do you mean?"

"I was around when Sean had his car wreck. I never thought I would see him drink again or have this kind of anger. It's like he's changed places with another person."

Caitlyn had seen signs that Sean was struggling with something but not to this extreme. She'd thought it had been grief over his father dying. Caitlyn had tried to talk to him about Andrew's death. He'd refused, and after that, Sean had avoided her. He stopped going both to church and to the Longhorn Cattlemen's Association meetings and functions, two groups he'd been very involved in.

Ian joined them in the hall. "Knowing Sean and his aversion to hospitals, I doubt the paramedics will get him to agree to go."

"I think we should stay awhile and see how he does. I'll call Granny and Emma to let them know what's going on."

Relief settled over Alice's face. "I doubt you two have eaten dinner yet. I can fix you some food. It'll give me something to do besides worrying."

One of the EMTs came out into the corridor. "He insists he's gonna stay here, and he wants us to leave. We can't force him to go to the hospital. We dressed the cut on his temple. His head hurts, but he says his vision is clear and he isn't dizzy. If he has symptoms like nausea, blurred vision, trouble with his balance or he's bothered by light or noise, he needs to see a doctor. He should get a few stitches as soon as possible. The laceration's likely to leave a scar."

"Thanks," Ian said as the other paramedic exited the room.

"I'll walk you to the door." Caitlyn started down the hall with the two EMTs, praying that Ian could talk some sense into his brother. There was a time they'd been close. She hated hearing they weren't now.

After the paramedics departed, Caitlyn dug into her purse where she'd left it, on the round table in the middle of the foyer. She found her cell phone and noticed a call from Granny. She hurriedly returned it.

"I'm sorry, Granny, for not calling earlier, but we came to see Sean and he was injured. The paramedics just left."

"What happened?"

Caitlyn told her how she and Ian found Sean. "Is Emma there?"

"Yes, we were hoping to talk y'all into eating dinner with us."

"Let her know about Sean. We'll stay here for a while. Alice is fixing us something to eat. I'll give you an update later. Tell Emma that Sean will be all right."

"Will he?"

"If Ian has anything to say about it, yes." It was one of the reasons she cared so much for Ian. He didn't give up on people.

"And that young man is mighty determined. He reminds me of you. Y'all always got along well, like a couple."

Was Granny trying to get her and Ian together? She was one of the few people who knew what had happened that summer after high school graduation. "Talk to you later, Granny. Bye."

What would have happened between her and Ian if she hadn't told that other guy she'd been dating that she just wanted to be friends? She'd seen a future with Ian and hadn't wanted any distraction as they took their relationship beyond friendship. But the consequences of that final date with Byron had left her shattered.

When Ian entered Sean's room after the paramedics left, his brother was curled onto his right side away from the door. Quietly, he rounded the end of the bed to see if Sean was awake. His brother's eyes were closed. Ian couldn't tell if he was asleep or just faking it. Ian decided to give Sean space and time to sober up.

Ian walked from the room, leaving the door open. Since the lock was busted, Sean couldn't barricade himself inside like before. His brother needed to face the problems that had led him to this point, but Sean would never listen to him. Ian hoped he would listen to Caitlyn. What he witnessed earlier was a plea for help, even if his brother wouldn't admit it.

He was glad that Caitlyn had been here, ready to offer her support. When they were growing up, she'd always been there for him, and that hadn't changed. He didn't realize how much he'd missed her. Most of his professional life had been spent solving others' problems, but he needed help with his brother. But with Sean he couldn't be objective. He hoped Caitlyn could.

Ian went downstairs and found her with Alice in the kitchen. The table was set for three, and the housekeeper placed a large serving dish of stew on it. "I know you can work wonders, Alice, but there's no way you had time to whip up this dinner." He inhaled deeply. "That smells delicious."

Alice grinned. "It's Sean's favorite. I made it earlier. I thought that would get him out of his room. It didn't, but I'm glad it's not going to waste."

"No way. I'll take some home with me for later this week." Ian caught Caitlyn's attention. "Have you had Alice's stew before?"

"No, but the smell was what drew me to the kitchen." Caitlyn took a seat at the table across from where Ian stood. "I talked with Granny. She'll let Emma know that Sean's okay. How was he when you left?"

"Asleep—I think." Ian pulled out the chair for Alice and scooted it in after she sat.

The housekeeper's cheeks reddened. "It's been a while since a man did that for me."

"That's the least I can do. I love Nana, but she doesn't cook nearly as well as you."

Alice picked up the bowl, scooped the stew onto her plate, then passed it to Caitlyn. "Ian, are you going to stay at your grandma's, come here or find your own place?"

He dished out his serving, then set the container in the middle of the table. "I've thought about living in the foreman's house here at the ranch since Bud doesn't, but first I want to make sure Nana is okay by herself because I don't think she'll want to move from her place, especially with Sally next door."

"Granny and Emma are usually together most of the time at one of their places. They help each other. I've heard from both of them that they don't want to move."

He would do whatever was best for his grandmother, but he was used to living alone. Over the years, he'd

become set in his ways—coming and going whenever
he needed to because of his job. Crime happened at all
hours of the day, and Nana tended to worry a lot. "Have
they ever talked about living together in one place?"

"About once a month. So far neither one is willing
to give up her house to move in with the other." Caitlyn took a bite of the stew. "Mmm! Wonderful, Alice."

She blushed. "Thanks. It's always nice to hear that."

"Sean and I have been a big fan of your cooking since
we were teenagers," Ian said.

Alice stared at her plate for a long moment, then
looked at Ian. "Lately he hasn't been a big fan of anything. Caitlyn, I hope you and Ian can help him."

"When was the last time he went to the doctor?"
Caitlyn clasped her glass and sipped the cold water.

"A couple of years, before Andrew passed away.
Sean was breaking in a horse, and the animal won that
round. I didn't think he'd go with the paramedics tonight, especially when Andrew left in an ambulance
and never came home."

"Is that when you began seeing a lot of changes?"

Alice cocked her head. "Yes, he found Andrew in
the office collapsed on the floor." Her forehead crin-
kled as she paused in thought. "I was going to say he
didn't leave the ranch much after that, but lately he has
been. I'd started wondering if he was seeing someone,
but this week everything went back to how it was right
after Andrew died."

Had his move back to Longhorn caused Sean to hole
himself up at the ranch? "What changed for Sean?"

Alice shrugged a shoulder.

"What kind of behaviors do you see the most, Alice?"
Caitlyn asked.

"Depression, losing interest in the ranch and, at times, escalating anger like tonight."

"I'll try again to talk with Sean when he isn't hungover. If I have to, I can come to the ranch to treat him."

"I hope he'll open up to you, Caitlyn." Ian's gaze connected with hers. She was such a caring person. That was one of the things that drew him to her even as teenagers. He missed being around her. "Sean probably won't be in any mood to talk tonight. I'll take you to your grandmother's. With all that's happened today, she'll want to see you."

"Are you sure you don't want me to stay?"

"Yes. I'm going to come back to the ranch and plop myself down in the stuffed chair in Sean's room. If he wakes up, I'll know. I'm a light sleeper."

When Ian finished his stew, he and Caitlyn cleared the table and rinsed the dishes so Alice could go to bed. Then Ian went upstairs to check on Sean. His brother hadn't moved from his previous position.

As Ian escorted Caitlyn to his SUV, she took his hand as though she could read his mind and the turmoil boiling in it. He felt her support without a word from her. He hadn't realized how important that was to him—until now. He opened the passenger door for her, then walked around to the driver's side. He should have come home months ago, but the Texas Ranger position hadn't opened up until recently.

As he drove away from the ranch, he sliced a glance toward Caitlyn. "Thanks for coming. I'm at a loss on how to help Sean. Any suggestions?"

"He needs to see his doctor and have a physical to rule out any kind of medical problem causing the personality change. And he needs to be in therapy. He's trying to deal with depression on his own. It's not uncommon for a depressed person to turn to drugs and alcohol to try and alleviate it. Of course, it only makes the situation worse. If he doesn't want to talk with me, I can recommend a therapist in Dallas."

"Any help is appreciated. I hope tomorrow morning Sean and I can have a civil conversation about what happened today."

"Today has been intense. I hope I make sense on the radio in the morning."

"Which days do you do your show?"

"Monday, Wednesday, Thursday and Friday. They want me to go to five days a week, especially as more stations are being added. I'm getting calls now from all over the States, but I volunteer at Matthew's Ministries on Tuesday and don't want to give that up."

Ian braked at a four-way stop sign. "You could always volunteer on the weekend."

"True. But I don't know if I want to take more on. I have patients I need to serve first. They're my priority. I'm stretching myself as it is, doing four days."

He pressed the accelerator and crossed the intersection. "Speaking of your patients, is there anyone who could be the caller?"

Caitlyn didn't answer for a long moment. "I have a few clients that have a lot of issues, but no one has mentioned Jane recently."

"How about in the past?"

"It's possible, but I'll have to search my case notes. I won't break patient-doctor confidentiality. It's important that my patients feel what they say to me will stay with me. I'm going to see the Shephards to let them know what you want. I can't imagine them not agreeing to me talking to you. As I said before, I don't see anything Jane said to me that would lead to someone murdering her."

"Thanks. You never know what sets a person off." Ian parked in Sally's driveway behind Caitlyn's Thunderbird. "I hope you're staying here tonight."

"I am. Granny wants me to. Emma is staying too."

"That's good. Otherwise, I doubt she'd sleep much since I'm going to be at the ranch. And I know I'll sleep much better knowing she's with y'all."

This time as he strolled up to Sally's house, he took Caitlyn's hand. He'd liked the earlier physical connection. He remembered as a kid going on a hike in the woods with Caitlyn and, because she feared stepping on a snake, he'd held her hand. That feeling of being her protector made his chest swell, even though he didn't know at the age of eleven what he would have done if they had encountered a snake.

"What are you smiling about?" she asked when she reached the porch illuminated with a bright light.

"Just thinking about the time we went hiking in Longhorn Woods, and you were afraid you'd see a snake."

"I'm still scared of snakes—all kinds."

Before she had a chance to ring the bell, the door opened. "It's about time you got here. Emma and I are having a hard time staying up." Sally moved away from the entrance and planted herself next to Nana.

His grandmother's arms were crossed over her chest and a formidable look on her face plainly showed her concern. "With a murderer running around town, I was getting worried."

"Nana, we're fine. We were in the house at the ranch

or in my car driving here. Besides, I'm trained to deal with dangerous situations."

"Is Sean still all right?" His grandma's intense expression eased.

"He's sleeping. If something changes for the worse, I'll let you know. I'll be staying there tonight."

Sally yawned. "Well, now that Caitlyn is here, we can go to bed."

"Yes, y'all go to sleep. I'll lock up the house." Caitlyn hugged her grandma and his.

As they shuffled toward the hallway to the bedrooms, Ian waited until they reached their destination before saying, "I'll walk through the house and make sure everything is locked down tight. There were times at Nana's that I'd find a door or window unlocked."

"It's a shame we even have to lock up at all. Years ago, people didn't in Longhorn."

"I know. But it's the reality now in our society."

Caitlyn strolled beside him while he went through the house. "You must have seen all the reasons why that's our reality. Being a therapist is hard, but I can't imagine what ugliness and evil you've encountered in your job."

As he moved from a door to a window, he thought about his fifteen years in law enforcement. "There have been times I've considered walking away, but then something like a case I worked on in December would make me realize I make a difference in people's lives, like you do with counseling."

"What happened in December?"

"I was part of a team that saved the lives of a woman and a baby. Also, I helped break up a drug cartel and take some seriously bad men down. That case was a success. I wish all of them were."

Caitlyn turned toward him, halting his step. "I hope Jane's murderer can be brought to justice. After my show tomorrow, I'm paying the Shephard family a visit. I worked on Jack's campaign the last two times. And if there is anything I can do to help with the case, I will."

"I appreciate the offer, but I don't want you involved. I don't want the killer to contact you again."

"What if I could help him?"

"How? Talk him into turning himself in? I don't think so."

Caitlyn straightened her shoulders and lifted her chin. "It's not unheard of. Police convince criminals to confess whenever they can."

"That's different. They're trained to protect themselves and others."

"And I'm trained to understand the reasons behind a person's actions, whether logical or illogical."

Ian headed for the entry hall. "I need to get back to the ranch. As much as I don't want to, I'm going to wake Sean a couple of times tonight and make sure he's all right. I worry about him slipping into a coma."

"You're brave. It'll be like poking a sleeping grizzly bear."

He chuckled, the tension from a moment ago evaporating. "Now that image will be in my mind when I do."

"You'll call me tomorrow and let me know how things are going?"

Her question made his spirits soar. "I look forward to talking to you."

And the smile she gave him as he left the house sent his heartbeat racing.

On the drive to the ranch, Ian recalled different times they'd spent together, especially as teenagers. He knew the exact moment Caitlyn became more than a friend— at a New Year's Eve party in her senior year in high school, when he'd kissed her at midnight. The connection had surprised him. After that he'd begun looking at her in a different light—as more than just a friend. But they'd been young, and life hadn't changed them yet.

At the ranch, Ian parked in front of the house and let himself in. Silence welcomed him. The grandfather clock chimed midnight. He'd been gone longer than he'd thought. He took the stairs two at a time.

As he entered his brother's bedroom, lit dimly by a single lamp, his gaze went immediately to the bed. Sean had turned over onto his back, half the covers thrown off him. His chest rose and fell gently. He looked peaceful now.

Ian sank into the lounge chair. Tired but not sleepy, he reclined and closed his eyes for a moment. He didn't want his brother to wake up alone. Something was wrong with Sean. The first thing he would do was persuade his brother to see a doctor. The man in the bed wasn't anything like he used to be. They had been close growing up. What had happened?

The bed creaked.

Ian opened his eyes to find Sean wrestling with his sheets. He immediately stood and hurried to his brother.

The thrashing increased.

Ian grabbed his shoulders and held him still. "Sean? Sean, what's wrong?"

"Why, Jane?" tore from Sean's mouth in anguish.

Did his brother even know she'd been killed? The

news didn't carry her death until the afternoon, and according to Alice, Sean had been holed up in his room.

"Jane!"

"Sean, wake up."

Sean's eyes bolted open and stared up at Ian. Then his brother blinked and yanked himself away from Ian.

"What are you doing here?" Sean asked in a clear, coherent voice, roughened with anger.

"Making sure you're all right after hitting your head." Ian straightened but stayed at the side of the bed. "Why were you calling Jane?"

Sean's forehead scrunched. "I don't know." He pulled the sheet up and over his shoulders, then rolled over partway until his back was to Ian. "Go home. I'm fine."

"I'm not leaving." He stood by the bed, waiting for his brother to say something more.

After five minutes, Ian circled to the other side to find Sean was asleep—or at least he thought he was. Ian returned to the lounge chair. He was staying, no matter what his brother said. This was his ranch too, and his brother needed him.

As the hour passed, Ian's eyelids became heavier and soon he fell sleep.

Four chimes sounded through the house.

Ian jerked awake. When he looked toward the bed, it was empty.

Where was Sean?

He scrambled to his feet, rushed into the hallway and searched every room except Alice's. Then he headed outside and went to the barn. No sign of Sean.

Was his truck still at the ranch?

Ian jogged to the garage and stared at the empty

place where Sean's truck should have been. His brother was in no condition to drive.

Why did he leave? More importantly, where did he go, and why did he say Jane's name last night?

Wearing the same clothes as yesterday, Caitlyn couldn't wait to get home, take a shower and change her outfit. She entered the kitchen where she heard Emma and Granny talking. The scent of coffee spiked the air, and she desperately needed caffeine. She hadn't slept well last night.

"Good morning." Caitlyn crossed to the counter and filled a mug with her grandma's special brew. "I wish I could stay, but I have to go by my house before the office."

"You should eat breakfast." Granny rose. "I can fix you something. Scrambled eggs with cheese is high in protein and fast to cook."

"Sorry. A shower is what I need. I'll grab an egg burrito on the way to work." She kissed Granny's cheek then Emma's. "I'll return your mug later today."

Before they tried to persuade her to stay, Caitlyn hurried outside into the crisp air. She unlocked her Thunderbird, slipped behind the steering wheel and backed out of the driveway. After yesterday, she would always lock her car and put the top up, even if it was at her grandmother's or her own house.

With the distance only three miles to her place, she pulled up to her home six minutes later, looking forward to a hot shower to chase away the early-morning chill. She walked up the sidewalk to her redbrick town house. She dug into her purse for her house keys.

When she retrieved them, she glanced up and opened

her door. Inside, she turned to shut it and froze. Pinned to the wood with a knife was a photo of a prone woman with her arms folded across her chest—just like the one of Jane.

FOUR

For a few seconds paralysis held Caitlyn in its grip, making it difficult to breathe.

What if the killer is still here?

The question prodded her to move—fast. She fumbled for the doorknob, turned it and fled her house. When she sat behind her steering wheel with the doors locked and the key in the ignition, she finally dug into her purse and withdrew her cell phone. Her hand shook as she punched in Ian's number. Her attention focused on her surroundings in case...

"Hi, Caitlyn. I'm on my way to your grandmother's house. Are you there?"

Ian's voice sent a surge of relief that she could get hold of him. She inhaled a deep breath then said, "No. He was in my house. Could still be there."

"Who?"

"The killer." She rushed through her explanation of what she'd found pinned to her door. Her chest rose and fell rapidly.

"Where are you?"

"In my driveway in my locked car."

"I'm not far away. Leave right now. I'll check your place."

"I'll start the car, but I'm not leaving. If he's still inside, I hope you can trap him. I want him to know I'm watching." She turned the key in the ignition.

"I'd argue with you, but I'm five minutes away. I'm placing you on hold while I call this in, then I'll be back."

The time she waited for him to return to her call seemed like ten minutes. Her heartbeat still pounded rapidly, its pulsating beat echoing in her ears.

"Caitlyn, are you still there?"

"Yes."

"Did you recognize the woman in the photo?"

She tried to picture the body. For a few seconds, she thought it was another picture of Jane, but it wasn't. A chill flashed up her body. "It's Kelli Williams. She's a patient of mine." The realization that Kelli was a victim, most likely connected to Jane's murder, sent a shudder down her, robbing her of any more words.

A movement out of the corner of her eye caught her attention and slammed her heart rate into overdrive. Her cell phone slipped from her fingers. She plunged her hand into her purse and withdrew her gun.

"I'm turning onto your street. Backup is right behind me." At the far end of Blue Bonnet Lane, Ian glimpsed the rear of the Thunderbird but, because of the neighbor's hedge, he couldn't see the whole car or Caitlyn in it.

It sounded as though the cell phone had been dropped—then silence.

"Caitlyn, are you all right?" Several seconds passed. "Are you okay?" he shouted into his phone.

Thoughts that the killer had her iced his blood. Fear dominated him, but he couldn't let it. He couldn't let anything happen to her.

As he closed the distance between them, Ian increased his speed. Seconds later, he slammed on his brakes and stopped right behind her car. Caitlyn wasn't in her vehicle. As he hopped from his SUV, he drew his gun, his gaze sweeping the area, then returning to the red Thunderbird.

Caitlyn popped up behind the steering wheel, holding her phone to her ear and threw a glance over her shoulder.

Relief surged through Ian, and he marched toward the driver's-side door and wrenched it open. She scrambled from her car while his gaze traveled down her length. Slowly his heartbeat returned to normal, but then he caught sight of a gun in her hand.

"What happened? I thought—"

Before he could finish what he was going to say, she threw her arms around him. Her body shook against him. While scanning the yard, he pressed her even closer and cherished the feel of her in his embrace—safe. Her spicy scent teased his nose, and he took several deep breaths.

Finally, her trembling subsided, and Ian leaned back to look into her face. Again he asked, "What happened?"

"I saw something moving out the corner of my eye, and I quickly reached for my purse where I keep this." She held up her small gun. "I looked around and only saw my neighbor's tomcat, so I searched for my cell

I'd dropped. It had slipped under the passenger's seat. When I sat up, you'd pulled up behind me. I've never been so glad to see someone."

"Me too. I was imagining all kinds of things." He glanced at two patrol cars arriving, sobering him to the reason Caitlyn had called him. "I'm going inside with one of the officers, while the other stays outside with you."

Caitlyn looked at the two policemen approaching, leaned closer to Ian and whispered, "I'd rather go with you. They can't have been on the force very long."

The urge to shelter and protect her inundated Ian. He was used to doing that but not with someone he cared about. He couldn't shake the fear that had swamped him, threatening his ability to do his job when he thought she'd been taken by the killer. He couldn't let personal feelings interfere with his professional duties. In his job, he'd always been able to separate the two, but he was afraid he wouldn't be able to with this case. "You'll be safer out here." He plucked the gun from her hand. "Without this."

"When I bought this gun in college, I took lessons. I know how to shoot, and I have a license to carry."

"But it makes police nervous." After slipping the small weapon into his pocket, Ian motioned for the two officers to join him.

"I want it back. It's for my protection."

The frantic ring to her words made Ian pause. "Protection? I'm here to help you."

"I can take care of myself."

Had something happened to Caitlyn? "*I* will. Let me check your house out first."

She nodded.

When the officers joined them, Ian told them about the photo inside, then he had one of the officers escort Caitlyn to the patrol car, while he walked with the second one to the front porch to collect the evidence and clear the town house. They both donned latex gloves.

Every scent sharpened as he entered Caitlyn's home. Clearing a place where a suspect might be hiding was dangerous. When he closed the door and spied the photo, he pulled out a couple of evidence bags and dropped the switchblade into one. Then, after studying the woman in the photo, he placed the image into the other bag. He noticed on the back of the picture were the words *Stop me!* written in red.

"Let's clear the house, then call the police chief. I'm working with the sheriff on a case that's connected to this photo." Ian went first, with the officer protecting his back.

Where was Kelli Williams's body? The killer had murdered Jane somewhere different from where she'd been dumped. The photo of her in Caitlyn's car had been staged just like Kelli's was. A serial killer? What other things did Jane and Kelli have in common, besides being Caitlyn's patient? Why was he leaving these pictures for Caitlyn? Was she going to be next?

Caitlyn sat in the front passenger seat while the young policeman stood guard by the hood, his hand near his weapon. The sight reinforced how dangerous the situation was. What if the killer was still inside? Each minute she waited for Ian and the other officer to emerge seemed like a lifetime.

She was supposed to have had a session with Kelli this afternoon. So much had happened since yesterday, when the killer called in. Would he again? Was there a way she could stop the murders? Could she persuade him to turn himself in? What if she couldn't and another person was killed?

I don't want this burden.

As the front door opened, Caitlyn sat up straight, her hands clenched in her lap. The officer appeared first, then Ian, talking to someone on his cell phone. She scrambled from the patrol car and headed for him.

Ian stopped halfway across the yard, finished his call, then slipped his phone into his pocket. She couldn't read anything in his expression. Her attention fell on the two evidence bags he held. As much as she wished this whole incident had been a dream, the sacks declared otherwise.

"No one was inside?" she asked, although she knew the answer.

He shook his head. "I saw how he got into your house, though. He broke a window in the back door and unlocked it. Your security system was disabled. It's an old system. You need to upgrade."

"I didn't even realize the alarm hadn't beeped when I came into the house." She swallowed several times, trying to wet her dry throat. "This has shaken me up." The vulnerability she'd experienced with Byron engulfed her, even after seventeen years. It made her angry because she'd thought she had dealt with it.

"I don't want you staying here. I'm having your house processed for fingerprints. I'll need yours to compare with what we find and anybody else's that has been to your place within the past few months. The sheriff is on his way and will take care of that, since it's related to our current case."

"Can I go in and get some clothes?"

"Yes, but I'll go with you." He passed her a pair of latex gloves. "Even with these on, only touch what you absolutely need to get what you're taking to Nana's. Both you and Sally need to stay there, and when I'm not around, a deputy or police officer from the Longhorn department will be with you."

"I still have to see my patients and do my show."

"Can you take a vacation until we catch this guy?"

"No. I have people who count on me. I can't let this killer dictate my actions. I want you to use me to draw this man out."

"No way! I don't want to find a photo of you." His neutral expression altered, reinforcing his vehement tone of voice.

"You won't, and I can help with the case. For some reason, he's targeted two of my patients. I can help you find a correlation between the victims. Jane is a young woman from a wealthy family, while Kelli is fifty and works at the grocery store as a clerk. At the moment, I can't figure out what they have in common."

"They have *you* in common."

"You think the killer is targeting my patients?" The very idea struck a deep chord of fear in her. Why would he pick her?

"It's a possibility and one I need to look into."

"Then I can help you for sure. If someone is targeting my patients, I need to assist you. This afternoon, I was going to see Jane's parents about opening their daughter's file. I can ask Kelli's daughter the same thing."

"As soon as Tom arrives, I'm going to check where Kelli lives. So far, no one has reported her missing. I'll need to talk to her employer, neighbors and daughter to figure out when she was taken."

"Okay. I'm calling my office and canceling my appointments this morning. I should come with you, especially to see her daughter, Allison. I just need to be at the station at ten thirty. I don't want to miss the show in case the killer contacts me again today."

"Good. I'll be there too, and if he phones, I can try to trace the call." Ian walked to his SUV and locked the evidence bags in a compartment in the back.

When the sheriff pulled up to her town house, Ian covered the distance between them and spoke to him, then returned to his car. "Okay, let's go. I told him what I was doing. I'll check in with him later. Do you know Kelli's address?"

She climbed into his vehicle. "Not off the top of my head, but I can call the office and get it."

"Good. Does her daughter live with Kelli?"

"No, down the street from her."

"Does she have a key to Kelli's house?"

"I don't know, but I can find out. I'll call her."

"Please do that, but don't tell her about the photo."

"Why not? She needs to know." Caitlyn sat forward, preparing to leave the SUV.

Ian moved closer to her, bent his head into the interior and said in a quiet, patient voice, "I never inform a person of a death in the family over the phone. I know in this case we don't have a body, but it isn't a conversation to have over the phone."

Caitlyn scooted back in her seat. "Allison will want to know why I'm asking her to bring her mother's key."

"Then since she lives down the street from her mother, don't call ahead. We'll go to her place first."

"Okay," Caitlyn murmured.

She watched Ian back away and skirt around the car's hood, his features set in what she was discovering was his professional face. There was no fear or anger in his expression. In fact, she couldn't read anything he might be contemplating. For a therapist, she spent a lot of her time understanding what a person was thinking about, especially if he was troubled. Body language was a tool she used a lot. But with Ian, she felt shut out, and that hurt. They hadn't seen each other in years, and she hadn't realized how much she'd missed him—until now. He used to be open, especially with her. Was this what his job had done to him? Or was it something else?

Ian approached Allison Walker's home, a small brick house with white trim, half a block away from her mother's place. Like the sheriff, this part of his job was his least favorite. Slanting a look at Caitlyn, he was glad she was with him. From all he'd heard about her, she was very good at her job as a therapist, counseling others in pain or fear.

When he reached the porch, he pushed the doorbell, and chimes echoed through the house. "I hope she can give us some leads. The family will need closure."

The door swung open. A young woman, her short dark hair streaked with purple, glanced from Ian to Caitlyn. "Why are you here? Is something wrong with Mom?" she asked her.

"Allison, this is Texas Ranger Ian Pierce, and he needs to talk to you about your mother. We can't get hold of her."

Ian tipped the brim of his white cowboy hat. "Ma'am, I'm sorry we have to meet this early, but I've come into possession of a photo of your mother. I suspect she's missing, possibly dead. I need you to confirm it's her."

Allison's eyes grew round as Ian put a pair of gloves on and carefully removed the picture from its evidence bag. He held it up for her to study.

She immediately said, "That's her. I thought she went to Fort Worth to see a friend for a couple of days. Did you take this photo? Where? What…" As her words tumbled from her, tears formed in her dark eyes and rolled down her face.

Caitlyn handed her a clean tissue from a travel packet. "May we come inside?"

The young woman dabbed her cheeks. "Of course." She stood to the side, then closed the door after them. "Let's sit in the living room. Excuse the mess. Before school, the kids were supposed…" Allison collapsed on the couch, dropping her head into her hands.

Caitlyn sat next to her and put her arm around her, while catching Ian's eye. She mouthed *Can I tell her?*

He nodded and took a seat across from them.

Caitlyn fumbled for her travel packet of tissue in her purse and gave Allison another one. "I found it attached to my door about an hour ago. I don't know why. I was supposed to have a session with your mother this afternoon. She never called to cancel her appointment. Why did you think she was going to Fort Worth for a few days?"

Allison looked up, her eyes glassy and red. "She talked about it at the end of last week. She had a few days off and didn't want to stay in town. She wanted to get away for a while. Her boss has been on a rampage."

"Rampage? What was he doing?" Ian asked, taking out a pad and pen.

"It's a she, and she was going through a 'nothing pleased her' phase. Nell Baker does that from time to time. Usually she's a great boss. Mom was hoping when she returned to work she would be over it."

Ian made a note to interview Nell Baker. "But you don't know if she left or not?"

"No, but her car was gone, so I assumed she did. It's usually parked in the driveway."

"When was the last time you talked to your mother?"

"Monday evening." Allison turned to Caitlyn. "She wouldn't miss her appointment without calling you to cancel. You've been helping her so much. She was asserting herself more, after years of my dad belittling her."

"May I have your permission to share with Texas Ranger Pierce your mother's information concerning her sessions with me? He's heading up the investigation."

Allison turned back to Ian. "I'll do anything to help you find my mom. Maybe she was only knocked out in the photo. Maybe..." More tears flowed when it seemed to dawn on Allison that wasn't what happened.

Ian leaned forward, resting his elbows on his thighs. "Your mother's case is tied with Jane Shephard's."

Allison gasped. "The one who was found dead yesterday morning?"

Ian nodded. "Does your dad live here?"

"He left Longhorn six months ago when my mother divorced him. I haven't heard from him. We weren't close."

"Besides your father, is there anyone who had a problem with your mother?"

Allison grabbed another tissue and patted her eyes. "No."

"Did she know Jane Shephard?"

"Not that I know of."

He'd hoped for a connection between the two women other than Caitlyn. "Would you please call your mother's friend in Fort Worth and see if she came to see her?" He prayed she was with her friend but, in his gut, he knew she wasn't.

Allison shot to her feet. "Yes! She may be there. Maybe someone faked the photo." She retrieved her cell phone from her jeans pocket and punched in the numbers. "Doris, is Mom there? I need to talk to her."

Ian didn't need to hear Doris's side of the conversation. Allison's brief hope drained from her face seconds later, and she sank down onto the couch. Caitlyn put her arm around the young woman as she finished the brief call.

"Mom decided at the last minute not to go and stay at home to rest. She spoke to Doris late Monday night after I phoned Mom."

"What time?" Ian asked.

"Eleven o'clock."

After jotting down the time, Ian put away his notebook and rose. "Have you gone to your mother's house since you talked to her on Monday night?"

Allison shook her head.

"Can you let us into her home?"

"Yes. Let me get the key."

When Allison left the living room, Caitlyn stood. "I was hoping that Kelli was with her friend."

"So was I." Ian moved toward the foyer. "It looks like Kelli was the first victim."

"That we know about," she whispered as Allison joined them and gave Ian the key.

After walking the short distance to Kelli's house, Ian turned on the porch toward Caitlyn and Allison. "I'd like y'all to stay out here. Was your mother's car in the driveway or the garage on Monday night?"

"I don't know, but it wasn't in the driveway Tuesday morning when I took the kids to school. It could have been in the garage because it was forecast to rain. That was usually the only time she would park it inside." Allison took one of the wicker chairs while Caitlyn sat in the other one.

Ian inserted the key in the door and let himself into the house. He didn't know what to expect, so he removed his gun from its holster. What if Kelli was killed right after Jane, not before? Did the order of their deaths mean anything?

As he moved through the place, checking first the living and dining rooms, then the kitchen, everything seemed in place. He'd have Allison go through her mother's house after he'd finished a walk-through. He opened a door that he thought led to the garage, flipped on the light and scanned the empty space—again very neat and tidy.

Next he headed for the hallway that led to the bedroom. The first room appeared to be where Kelli worked on various arts and crafts projects. Beside it looked like a spare bedroom for guests. Finally, he approached one at the end of the corridor. The door was shut, while the others had been open.

When he stepped inside, he took in the chaos—a chair lying on its side, a lamp smashed, the dresser items on the floor. The scent from a broken bottle of perfume pervaded the room with a sickly aroma. Stepping farther in, Ian lifted his gaze to a mirror above the bureau and gritted his teeth at the words *Stop me!* written across it in what appeared to be blood.

FIVE

Caitlyn stared at the wall clock in the studio, the seconds slowly ticking by. Only five more minutes left of the show. Hadn't she done this yesterday, and the call after the final commercial had been the killer?

Through the glass, Melanie held up her fingers and counted to three.

Caitlyn leaned toward the mic and said, "I have time for one more caller." The panel lit up, and she reached for the button to punch, her hand trembling. "This is Caitlyn. You're on the air."

Silence.

Her heart pounded, and her palms were sweaty. She started to hang up, relieved she didn't have to talk to the killer, but before she could, a female voice said, "I never thought I would get through."

"Can I help you with anything?" Caitlyn relaxed in her chair.

"My boyfriend has been calling my best friend. What should I do?"

"Have you asked him why he's doing that or talked to your best friend?"

"Well, no. He'd know I was checking his phone."

"Why were you checking his phone?" Caitlyn's gaze latched on to Ian standing behind Melanie. His presence reassured her she would be safe.

"I... I don't trust him."

"Why is that?"

"Well..." The female guest caller sighed. "He's so popular and cute. I don't understand why he's dating me."

"Ask him. For a relationship to work, honesty between the partners and open communication are essential. You might ask him why he's dating you and let me know how your talk goes. You can either call back or email me." Caitlyn gave out her contact information she used for her show, then said the spiel for the end of the program.

She sat staring at the call board, a few lighting up, but when the hour was over, anyone trying to talk to her heard a canned reply about calling back another day. Had her last guest kept the killer from getting through? After seeing Kelli's bedroom and the mirror over the dresser, she was glad that he didn't call in or was too late.

Ian opened the door to the booth. "Ready? We need to meet with the Shephards before you go to your office."

"I only have two patients today, since Kelli..." She couldn't say the words.

"I'll be picking you up. If she showed up, that would be the best news, and I would gladly find something to keep me occupied while y'all talk."

"But that's not going to happen, is it?" Caitlyn gathered up her purse and briefcase, her shoulders drooping at the thought.

"No. Someone fought with her and took her from her house, using her car. The police statewide and in bordering states are looking for both her vehicle and Jane's."

"They could be hundreds of miles away by now."

"One of them will turn up unless he's not a lone operator." He opened the door into the hallway and waited for her to exit first.

"No, there's just one. His notes indicate that. It's a cry for help or a game to him."

As they left the building, Ian clasped her free hand. "The news about Kelli hasn't been released to the press yet. But it won't be long before it is. The sheriff has received a lot of calls about what was going on at your house and then at Kelli's. Tom has set up a press conference for later. I asked Allison not to say anything to anyone for the time being."

"We need the public's help on finding this killer. Maybe someone saw something and didn't know the seriousness of what's happening." Caitlyn didn't want him to release her hand, but they had a lot to do today. She let go and slid into the front seat of his SUV, the warmth of his palm against hers lingering.

"I hope someone has and will come forward." As he made his way to the other side of the car, he answered a call.

Caitlyn couldn't tell what was being said, but whatever it was had to be tied to the case because his forehead creased and his professional persona fell into place as he placed a call, then shoved his cell phone in his pocket.

When he settled behind the steering wheel, she asked, "What's wrong?"

"A car was set on fire at the Shephards' ranch in the

middle of a cornfield. That was Senator Shephard. It's southeast of the house, next to my family's property."

Caitlyn bent forward and looked in that direction. "I see dark plumes of smoke in the sky. Is it Jane's car?"

"He's not sure. They're trying to contain the fire before it spreads. I'm going to drop you at your office and have an officer stay with you."

"But what about me talking to the Shephards?"

"The senator mentioned doing it later."

"Let me know if it's Jane's car."

"I will, and I'll pick you up later this afternoon." He started the engine and pulled out of the parking lot by the radio station. "Officer Collins should be at your office by the time we arrive."

"Blake Collins?"

"Yes. Do you know him?"

"I've run into him from time to time." Should she tell Ian that she counseled his mother? Did Blake even know she did? Thankfully, Ada Collins wasn't one of her patients today.

"He'll be outside your office door in case there's a problem."

"That's fine."

Not fifteen minutes later, Caitlyn arrived at the clinic with a lunch she had grabbed at a fast-food restaurant. As she and Ian entered the building, Officer Collins approached them in the waiting room. Did he know that his father abused his mother? Lately, it had gotten worse. Ada was very good at hiding her injuries, and her son didn't live with them anymore. He had recently married a nurse who worked at the medical center nearby.

Caitlyn entered her personal office, while Ian told the

younger policeman his duties. Before Ian left, he swung her door open and popped his head through the gap.

"See you in a few hours. Maybe I'll have good news for you by then, but in the meantime you're surrounded by people you work with and know."

One of the things that bothered her the most was she might know the killer. She was beginning to look at the people around her in a different light. And that wasn't good if she was going to help others.

After he left, she quickly ate her sandwich and washed it down with a cup of iced tea. She only had a couple of minutes before her first afternoon patient, Missy Quinn, arrived. She hadn't been seeing her for long, but Missy suffered from depression, and presented as though she'd given up on life. Caitlyn suspected it was due to a trauma in her past she hadn't dealt with. She understood.

She greeted her client at the door and shook her hand. When she'd first come to therapy five months ago, Missy wouldn't touch anyone, even to shake hands. Caitlyn had visited Missy once at her home and saw evidence that she was married. Was her husband the cause of her fear and paranoia?

"How are you doing?" Caitlyn gestured for Missy to take her usual seat.

"I almost didn't come."

"Why?"

"Jane Shephard was killed yesterday."

"Were y'all friends?"

"No. Was she raped?"

"I don't know. Why do you want to know?"

Shrugging, Missy lowered her head and wrung

her hands in her lap. "She didn't live too far from me. Scary."

How would Missy react when she discovered there was another murder and Kelli lived a street over from her?

Ian stood next to Jack Shephard and the sheriff, and they waited until the fire department had extinguished the fire before they approached the Lexus. "Is this Jane's?"

Jack stared at the side of the charred vehicle with patches of blue showing in certain places. "Yes, I believe so. It's the right model and color."

Tom circled the car. "If they can get the VIN number off it, we'll know for sure. I'm going to have it towed to a garage we use. Someone went to a lot of trouble to destroy this car and any evidence we might have recovered from it."

"I'm putting up a fifty thousand dollar reward for any information that leads to a conviction." Jack turned away from the sight. "I can't believe there's another missing woman."

"Did Jane and Kelli Williams have any connection?" Ian stepped up to the passenger side and looked inside, then inspected the back seat. Anything inside had been destroyed. When the vehicle cooled, he hoped there might be evidence in the trunk that wasn't as charred.

"I don't think so. Kelli goes to the same church, but I never saw them together. You might ask my wife. She would know more about Jane's friends and her daily schedule, since I'm often at the state capitol."

"May Caitlyn and I reschedule our meeting to after five?" Ian stepped back and panned the isolated area of the Shephard ranch. Not far away was Longhorn Lake. Was that the way the killer drove the car onto the property?

"Yes. It would be better for Ruth and me. She's trying to make the arrangements for the funeral."

"When is the funeral?" Ian peered across the pasture that ran along the southwest border of his family's ranch. He stiffened when he caught sight of his brother sitting on a horse looking toward them.

"First of next week. We have family coming in."

The sheriff joined them. "We'll be posting a few deputies at the funeral."

"Do you really think the killer would make an appearance? If he did, he would regret it." The senator's eyes narrowed into a laser-sharp gaze. "It has to be a stranger. Everyone loved Jane. She's the one who ran our foundation and was always ready to help anyone who needed it."

"We're doing everything we can to find the killer. I'm going to follow the tire tracks to see where he drove the car onto your ranch." Ian followed the trampled corn crop to the back part of the pasture, glancing every once in a while toward his family's ranch.

Sean had disappeared. Why had he been there watching? Ian needed to confront his brother about murmuring Jane's name in anguish last night. He couldn't see Sean killing anyone, but then, if he'd started drinking again, there was no telling what his brother could be responsible for. He didn't want to jump to any conclusion about Sean, but it was hard not to. After talking to Nana early this morning, Ian had discovered Sean had been acting even more strange for the past couple of months than ever before.

Could Caitlyn help Sean? Would his brother take advice from him or anyone else?

He should have come home sooner. He'd known Sean wasn't dealing well with the stress of their father's death. Sean and his dad had been much closer than Ian had been with his dad.

Ian hopped over the fence onto the public land encircling the lake and tracked the tire prints to a gravel road about a hundred yards away. At least how the car ended up on the Shephard ranch had been answered, but why risk dumping it here? To make a point? What?

How about Kelli's missing vehicle? Would they find it on fire in some other field?

A rustling sound behind Ian caused him to put his hand on his gun and swivel around.

"What are you doing here?" Ian asked Sean who had dismounted his horse and tied him to the fence by the family's property.

"I saw the fire from the house and rode here to see what was going on. You know how dangerous a grass fire can be, especially since we haven't had that much rain lately. Why was Jane's car there?"

Earlier Ian had called Alice to see how Sean was doing and if he knew about Jane's death. He did. "Her killer most likely left it there and set it on fire. Some kind of statement maybe." Ian scrutinized the dark circles under Sean's eyes. Where had he gone early this morning? "Were you and Jane dating?"

Sean's slumping posture stiffened while his brother puffed out his chest. "What are you implying?"

"Last night you were murmuring Jane's name a few times. If she wasn't important to you, I doubt you would do that. I'm overseeing her murder investigation, and

I need all the information I can get to find her killer. Were y'all dating?"

Sean took his cowboy hat off and hit it against his leg. "No—yes."

"Which is it?"

"I *was* dating her."

"How long were you seeing her?"

Sean shrugged. "A couple of months."

"When did you start drinking?"

His brother pivoted. "This conversation is over."

"Why?"

At the fence of the Pierce ranch, Sean looked back and said, "None of your business."

"If I find you drinking and driving, I'll arrest you."

"Of course you would. You were always the good son."

Ian opened and closed his fists, realizing how desperate his brother had become.

As he watched his older brother ride back toward the barn, Ian couldn't shake the question: Could Sean kill these women, especially since he was drinking again and he was losing control? Possibly even blacking out? He wanted to say no, but he didn't know Sean anymore.

Lord, what do I do about Sean? How can I help him when he doesn't want it?

Caitlyn closed her notepad. "Paul, this has been a good session. A few months ago, you couldn't even talk about your childhood. Now you are. You're making progress."

"Not fast enough. I still can't sleep much at night. I keep thinking about what I did wrong during the day. Maybe my mother was right. I was a screwup."

"Keep a journal of what goes right during the day, then before you go to sleep read it to remind yourself you aren't making one mistake after another."

"What if I can't think of anything to write? Like this morning everything went wrong." Paul clasped his hands so tightly that his knuckles whitened.

"Were you at work on time?"

"Yes, I'm never late."

"That's one thing you can put down."

"Maybe." He frowned as he pushed to his feet. "I'll try what you said, but I don't think it will work."

"Be open to it. It may work."

Paul Nichols mumbled something under his breath that Caitlyn couldn't hear and shuffled toward the door. She was used to that. His negativity was a challenge for her as a therapist. She followed him to lock the door and tell Officer Collins he could leave. Ian was on the way to pick her up. She hated the idea of a policeman in the hallway. Every patient she'd seen this afternoon had asked about him, and she'd given them a vague reason. She prayed Ian had found a link between Jane and Kelli other than seeing her for counseling.

As her last patient left, Ian passed him in the corridor and nodded to him, and Paul hurried his pace. As Ian closed the space between them, Caitlyn noticed he looked worn-out. He couldn't have gotten much sleep last night while staying at the ranch to watch over Sean.

"Thanks, Officer Collins, for helping out." Ian paused next to Caitlyn.

"Come in. I'm taking some files home with me. Are we going to see Jane's parents?"

"Yes, I told Nana we would be at her house for dinner. Sally has taken a suitcase to my grandmother's house. You'll possibly be at Nana's for several days, maybe longer. Do you need anything else besides what you took this morning?"

The thought of the photo pinned to her front door sent a shudder down her. "I don't think so. Has the sheriff finished with my place?" She put what she needed into her briefcase.

"Yes. After dinner, you and I need to sit down and figure out any connection between the two women. Senator Shephard can't think of any other than church, but his wife will be meeting with us too. Maybe she'll know something."

Ian went out into the corridor first using her private office entrance and looked up and down the hall before signaling her to leave too. "It was Jane's car at their ranch, but there've been no sightings of Kelli's yet."

As they drove toward the Shephard ranch, Caitlyn stared at his family's main house while they passed the Pierce property. "How's Sean? Did you see him today, since you were so close?"

"Yes, he was watching them put out the fire."

She studied his stiff posture and hard profile. A tic in his jaw indicated he was clenching his teeth. "Do you think Sean has something to do with this?"

He released a long breath. "It has crossed my mind. He mumbled Jane's name last night in his sleep. I asked him about Jane, and he admitted they had been dating, but it had to be in secret because no one else knew."

"Why would they do that? Because Jack and Sean don't get along?"

"Probably. I got the impression when I talked with him that his last meeting with Jane didn't end well. Sean shut down when I questioned him too much."

"That doesn't surprise me. He's isolating himself from others and that might be the reason he was pulling away from Jane, or she was from him."

Ian stopped at an intersection. "I followed the tire tracks from Jane's car to the rear of the property. It wasn't too far from where the public land starts. I lost the trail at the gravel road my family put in to the back of our ranch. We have a gate to the field that borders the Shephards' land. There is dense vegetation in our pasture where a car could be hidden. What if Jane and Sean had a fight and—"

"Don't do that until you have evidence to support it. If someone hid the car back there, then possibly you'll find tracks."

"I know, but I don't want Sean to see me check it out. After we leave the Shephards' house, I'm going to drive around to the gravel road and see. I didn't have time earlier." He parked in front of a large three-story antebellum home.

But before he could open his door, Caitlyn grabbed his arm, stopping him from getting out. "Sean is troubled and angry, but that doesn't mean he would kill someone. I still think of the time the three of us used to play together. Remember when I fell into the pool, and I couldn't swim very well?"

"I couldn't either."

"He jumped in and, in spite of me fighting him in my panic, he brought me to the side of the pool when he wasn't much better than you or me. I believe that person is inside him." She rubbed her hand up and down his arm. What would have happened if they had continued dating that summer? Her throat closed at the lost opportunity. "You know you can talk to me about anything. There's nothing you can tell me I haven't heard before."

"How do you do it? Listen to your patients' problems?"

"I have to detach a part of myself in order to help them. It's one thing on paper, another to put into practice."

He faced her. "I know what you're talking about. I've had to learn to separate my professional life from my personal one. Coming back to Longhorn has made that difficult when I know many of the people involved."

She couldn't resist cupping the side of his face, wanting to wipe the perturbed look from his face, smooth away the worried creases on his forehead.

He pulled back and turned to exit the SUV. "The senator is standing in the entrance."

The heat of a blush singed her cheeks. The physical connection had felt good between them—at least for her. She scrambled from the car and hurried toward the porch. If only things had been different when she was eighteen.

"Come in. Ruth is in the living room." Jack stepped to the side while she and Ian entered the mansion.

Ian and Caitlyn settled into chairs across from the Shephards, who sat side by side on the couch, grief etching lines of fatigue into their faces.

"I'm so sorry about Jane. If I can do anything to help y'all, please let me know." Caitlyn crossed her legs and sat back somewhat, intending to let Ian lead the conversation.

But the senator leaned forward, clasping his hands. "I understand from the sheriff you found a photo in your car yesterday, and then this morning there was a picture of Kelli Williams, similar to—" he cleared his throat "—similar to Jane's, stuck to your front door with a knife. Apparently the blood on it indicates it's the weapon used to kill my daughter. In fact, the killer has been in touch with you through your radio program. Do you have any idea why he's targeting you?"

"His message is for me to stop him, but I have no idea who he is."

Jack scowled. "Could he want to make national headlines by contacting you on the radio?"

"I suppose he could, but he didn't call me today."

"I don't want my daughter's death turned into a circus and paraded before everyone. I just want this man found and for us to be allowed to mourn our loss privately." Ruth laid her hand over her husband's. "Our phone hasn't stopped ringing."

"I understand. We all want this settled quickly. That's why I'm here today. To see if you'll give me permission to discuss what Jane and I talked about in our sessions if I feel it's relevant to the case."

"No, absolutely not." The senator shoved to his feet and glared down at Caitlyn. "I didn't want her seeing you in the first place."

"Why?"

"Because we—her family—are here for her. She didn't need anyone else."

Ruth rose next to her husband and again took his hand. "Jack, if it can help find the killer, then we need to. Dr. Rhodes, I'm sure, especially with another murder, that Texas Ranger Pierce could just get a subpoena through a judge."

The senator backed away from his wife. "But we have no idea what Jane told her. If it's our private life,

I don't want everyone knowing it. The vultures in the press will dissect our lives. It's already bad enough being a public figure."

"Caitlyn, I know how much you helped Jane. I trust you in this. You have my permission to share what you think would help find the killer." Ruth sank onto the couch. "Can we help in any other way?"

"Yes," Ian said. "I already asked the senator if there was a connection between Jane and Kelli other than attendance at the same church. Do you know of another one?"

"The Shephard Foundation Jane oversaw. I remember seeing them together last Christmas. Kelli helped Jane with some of the fund-raisers, especially where the church was involved. But I think that was all."

"Thanks. If you think of any other connection, please let me know." Ian stood and looked at the senator. "Sir, I'll keep you informed about the investigation, and if y'all think of anything that might help the case, call me anytime."

Ruth walked them to the front door while her husband sat on the couch, his head dropped forward. "Please forgive Jack's outburst. This has hit him very hard."

Caitlyn gave Ruth a hug. "I understand. Remember, I'm here for you if you need to talk."

"Thank you." Unshed tears glistened in the older woman's eyes. "Good day."

Once Caitlyn settled into the passenger seat, the day finally caught up with her. She wasn't sure she could think rationally enough to discuss the investigation with Ian tonight and, as he slipped behind the wheel, he looked like he'd hit a wall too.

While he drove around to the gravel road between the ranches and the lake, silence ruled. When they got out, Caitlyn joined Ian, and they headed for the dense vegetation along the property line of the Pierce ranch. Halfway there, Ian grasped her hand. Her heart skipped a beat at his touch.

"When I was a kid, Sean and I used to build forts in the bushes."

"I remember you showing me one, but Sean wasn't happy you brought a girl to see it."

"He spent more time back here than I did, especially after our mom died. When he found her dead out in the field, he shut down. I don't think he's ever really opened up after that."

Caitlyn slid a glance toward Ian. She prayed Sean wasn't involved with what was going on. He had issues. If he didn't deal with them, they would send him down a path of self-destruction. Knowing Ian, he would blame himself for not being here for his brother.

Ian went first through the thick brush, the tree canopy overhead darkening their path. He stopped and withdrew a small flashlight, then proceeded.

This place would be a good dump site if the killer didn't want the body to be found right away. Immediately she thought about Kelli still missing and shivered.

He must have felt the tremor because Ian slowed and looked back at her. "Okay?"

"I don't remember this place being so dark and dense."

"It wasn't when we were growing up. It keeps people at the lake from wandering onto our ranch, so Sean has let it go. The fence for our southern property border is set in by five yards." Ian kept walking.

"Sean moved the fence?"

"No, my father did. It helps keep the cattle rustlers out."

As she peered all around at the vegetation, she began noticing broken branches. With her gaze fixed on the ground, she ran into Ian, who stopped suddenly. She leaned around him and stared where his flashlight illuminated the soft earth.

Tire tracks.

SIX

A faint, putrid scent invaded Ian's nostrils. The smell of death, something he would never forget or get used to. He lifted his flashlight, searching for the source. A few yards away was the rear of a black vehicle with Kelli Williams's license plate number.

Caitlyn gasped. "Is that Kelli's car?"

"Yes."

Putting her hand over her nose, she started forward. "She must be in it."

He turned around. "I want you to stay here. I need to check the car."

She nodded.

As Ian approached the four-door sedan, the rancid odor grew stronger, prompting his gag reflex. Pinching his nose and holding his breath helped, but nothing could completely get rid of the scent. He circled the car, noting that all the windows were rolled up. He shone the flashlight into the interior. No body. That left the trunk. He went back to the driver's side door and opened it. The keys were still in the ignition.

When he punched a button on the key fob, the trunk lid popped up. Inside was a small woman in her fifties, with short brown hair, dressed in pajamas. Kelli lay curled on her side, stab wounds in her back visible, the blood around the wounds dried. He shone his light in the trunk and couldn't find any other trace of blood. This wasn't the scene of her murder.

After taking a few photos with his cell phone, Ian returned to Caitlyn and moved farther away from the black car. "It's Kelli. I'm notifying the sheriff, and when he comes, I'll take you back to Nana's house and make sure an officer stays with you."

Ian called Tom and told the sheriff what he'd found and where. "Kelli wasn't killed in the car. We need to try to figure out from the photos where he's killing the women and posing them for the pictures before moving the bodies."

"From the photos you sent, it looks like a cabin," Tom said. "I'll have the pictures blown up as much as possible, and I'm sending a deputy to your grandmother's house. I think Caitlyn may be the key to this."

Ian's gaze latched onto Caitlyn, who stared at the car through the bush. "I agree. I'll stay until you can secure this scene." Ian disconnected the call and slipped his cell phone into his pocket.

"I have to see Allison. She needs to know her mother was found."

"We'll stop by her house on the way to Nana's." Even in the dim light, he could tell the color had drained from her face. Taking her hand, he moved them even farther away, positioning himself to keep an eye on the car but shielding her from the sight. Then he wrapped his arms around Caitlyn. "I'm sorry you're here. I didn't think that Kelli's car would be here."

She pressed herself closer to him. "I knew she was

dead. At least Allison will have an answer, which will help her in the long run." Trembling, she looked up at him. "I don't understand what's going on. Why is this killer leaving me notes to stop him?"

"I don't think he wants you to stop him. I think he's taunting you. You're at the center of this for some reason that might not make sense to us yet."

"But Kelli and Jane aren't friends and don't even come to see me on the same day. They don't interact at my office. They have occasionally at church but that doesn't have anything to do with me. That might be the real connection." Tears glistened in her eyes.

"I'm going to talk to the pastor. I have to consider every possibility." He tightened his embrace. "Tonight we'll talk about both. Maybe there's a link you haven't considered."

"I feel helpless. Not a feeling I like." She glanced back at the car and shuddered. "What if I'm the real target and the killer is…" Her voice thickened, and she closed her eyes, burying her face into the nook of his arm. "What have I done wrong?"

Her muffled speculation left a deep ache in his gut. He'd seen his share of victims who blamed themselves for what happened. The fearless girl he used to know wouldn't have done that. What changed? He wasn't going to let Caitlyn do that to herself. "Nothing. You didn't murder these women. He did. Remember that when you think you're in the wrong."

"I know you're right on one level, but my life has been dedicated to helping people and, at the moment, I don't feel like I am. And I certainly don't know how to help this killer."

"Kelli's daughter said you do help people. Focus

on that. You counsel people with problems. Tonight, we'll also need to start considering who might have a grudge against you." He rubbed his hand up and down her spine as though that would take the sting out of what he was implying. "You make a difference in your patients' lives, but there may be one you couldn't reach and he snapped."

"I'd hope I would be able to see that."

When the sheriff and three deputies arrived, Ian quickly stepped away from Caitlyn and filled Tom in on what he'd done so far. "I'll be back after informing the victim's daughter and taking Caitlyn to my grandma's. I believe Caitlyn somehow holds the key to who murdered these women. I don't want us sharing that with the press, though."

Tom nodded. "But I'll be warning all women in the area to be extra vigilant. I'll be working with Chief Franklin, and we'll piece this together."

When Ian rejoined Caitlyn, he took her hand and started for his parked SUV. "Let's go."

Halfway to his car, Caitlyn asked, "Why is he playing some kind of cruel game? Why didn't he just come after me, if I'm the true target?"

"We don't know that for sure yet. If we can figure out what his reason for toying with you is, we can probably come up with a short list of suspects."

"While right now it could be anyone. We came here because Sean said Jane's name last night in his sleep. What are you going to do about Sean?"

"Try to figure out what's going on. Get help for him." And pray it wasn't Sean. His brother didn't have a connection to Kelli—at least one he knew about.

Caitlyn stopped at his vehicle, leaning back against

the passenger door. "I wish he really wanted help to stop."

"So do I, but I don't think so." He stared at Caitlyn for a couple of seconds and, as though his hands had a will of their own, he cupped her face, wanting to take away the fear lurking in her eyes. He'd been in dangerous situations countless times but Caitlyn hadn't. He wanted to protect her and keep her shielded from the evil he'd seen as a law enforcement officer.

She lifted her big, worry-filled eyes to his. "I'd help him if he let me."

Ian bent his head closer to her. "I've missed…our friendship."

"I came back to Longhorn for good seven and half years ago and set up my practice. You're the one that moved all around. I had a hard time keeping up with where you were posted."

He couldn't tell her that once he became comfortable in a town, he moved on before he wanted to settle there—and possibly find a woman to share his life with. He'd tried that once, and it hadn't ended well. He couldn't let personal feelings get in the way of doing his job. "I'll be here for a while. As long as Nana and Sean need me."

Her gaze snagged his. "What if *I* need you?"

Her question prevented him from having a coherent answer. What did she mean by that? Years ago, she'd been the one who left Longhorn the summer after high school without any explanation, except for a message saying she needed to go to college a month early. She stayed away for a year before returning for school breaks and by that time he'd joined the Texas Highway Patrol and was assigned in Brownsville. For over seventeen years they'd rarely seen each other. He'd come into town. She would be gone. Had she been avoiding him all this time? If so, why?

Later that night, Caitlyn sat in a lounge chair at Emma's house and went through patient files on her laptop. She had more detailed ones in hard copy at her office, but they would be hard to transport to and from here, considering the number of cases she'd had.

The sound of footsteps disturbed the quiet, and she peered up as Ian entered the den. "Since you've been gone, I've read another patient's file out of hundreds."

"While I only have two." He eased into the other lounge chair on the right side of the end table between them. "Our grandmothers have gone to bed, and the house is locked up."

"What did the sheriff have to say?"

"Just filling me in on evidence collected from Kelli's car. Not much. Most surfaces were wiped clean. No fingerprints on handles, the trunk or the steering wheel."

"In other words, a dead end."

"Yep." Ian picked up Jane's file. "So far not a lot of physical evidence to tie anyone to either death. Nothing on the photos. And the words *Stop me!* were written differently on the two photos."

"Did you find Kelli's cell phone?"

"No, but wherever it is, it's turned off. I can't trace it. The same with Jane's."

"How about the switchblade at my house?"

"It was the murder weapon for Jane, but it's a common brand sold widely in stores and on the internet. Once the killer is apprehended, we can use the purchase of a similar switchblade as a piece of evidence at his trial. It looks like he used the same type on both women, although the knife from your house only had one blood type on it. The wounds match."

A dull ache pounded against her temples. "Who was killed first?"

"Kelli, by one day."

"Then why did I get a photo of Jane first?"

"If the person is trying to get attention, Jane's death would garnish more."

"Because of who her father is. Does that mean Jane was really the target and Kelli a trial run?"

"I don't know. Jane's body was disposed of more visibly. Chances were she would be discovered before Kelli, but I think her car and body were placed where she was found probably on Tuesday. It might even be the reason he burned Jane's car in a pasture near where Kelli was."

"So that could be important." Caitlyn massaged her temples, her eyes tired from staring at the computer screen most of the evening.

"Or not."

She swung her attention to him. "How do you do this day after day? How do you manage all the data?"

"This case is more complicated than others I've investigated. The sheriff is setting up a murder board with the victims and elements of evidence on it. I'm also going to do one here, since I'll be spending a lot of time here rather than my office."

When he looked at her, goose bumps covered her from head to toe. The intensity in his hazel eyes—more brown than green—made her feel safe and sad at the same time. Half a lifetime ago, she'd been a scared young woman who had fled Longhorn rather than tell anyone about what had happened to her. Later, she told Granny. She was the only person who knew.

"Have you found anyone you think is capable of these murders?"

"No, but I'm generalizing their psychological problems. There won't be any name attached to my description. I'm almost through the first year. This is time-consuming, but I have to protect my patients' privacy. Thankfully, tomorrow is Friday, and I'll have the weekend to finish going through the files."

"After you see your patients and do your show?"

"Yes. I have a full day tomorrow, starting at eight."

He chuckled. "I guess I'll miss my beauty sleep."

Their gazes linked across the short space that separated them. "Oh, I don't think you need that. You have enough beauty to put most men to shame."

His cheeks reddened. "Beauty? I object to that word."

"On the outside you're handsome, and on the inside you have a deep beauty about you."

His face flushed further with embarrassment, he lowered his head and fixed his attention on the file folder lying in his lap.

She laughed. "I can say that because I've known you many years."

"But not recently."

"You haven't changed from when you were a teenager. You fight for the underdog and believe in being fair, and that's not just in the past but the present too. I still remember when you stepped in at school when that ninth grader was being bullied by some seniors. You took them all on."

"And I got suspended along with them."

"But only for two days. They got a week."

"Okay. Break time is over."

Caitlyn tried to concentrate on the file she had in front of her. Missy Quinn. She'd been working with her for a few months, and she still hadn't gotten to the core of the young woman's condition. Lately, Missy had seemed close to telling her but would suddenly shut down before she did. It reminded Caitlyn of how she'd been at eighteen after going through trauma. For months, she wouldn't say a word to anyone about it. Only when she broke down and sobbed over the phone with Granny did she reveal she'd been raped by a guy she'd thought she'd known and liked. After that, she was able to get the counseling she needed to move forward.

After reviewing Missy's file, she wrote down a description on her notepad for Ian. People like Missy were why she'd become a therapist. Although she had a killer interested in her for some reason at the moment, she wouldn't change her career for something safer.

When Caitlyn finished the last file for the past year, she needed to get up and stretch. Her back hurt, and all her muscles felt stiff. She rose and raised her arms above her head, then twisted from side to side.

"There aren't enough hours in the day to get everything done." Ian set Kelli Williams's folder on the end table. Then he too stood. "The only possible lead from what I read about Kelli is her ex-husband."

"I agree he would be a good candidate for her. He wasn't happy at all when she finally filed for divorce. Thankfully for Kelli, the company he worked for transferred him to a new position, and he moved away from Longhorn six months ago."

"Do you know where?"

"To Atlanta, according to Kelli, but you should see if

Allison knows if he's still there. I spent the past months with Kelli building up her self-esteem, and she was making good progress." Caitlyn remembered the older woman's smile their last session when she told Caitlyn about her work with the Shephard Foundation. "Kelli helped with the foundation and got a lot out of volunteering, but why would Clark Williams murder Jane, especially after his ex-wife?" She arched her back to try to coax the last of the stiffness from her body.

"Sometimes a killer's motive doesn't make sense to others. Here." He drew a circle in the air. "Turn around."

After she did, he put his hands on her shoulders and kneaded the tightness created by sitting hunched over her work for hours. "Perfect. Until I stood, I didn't realize how stiff I was. I always get up and walk around my office between patients." She glanced back at him, not realizing how close his head was to her—only inches apart.

His lime-scented aftershave overwhelmed her senses and stirred feelings in her from when he'd brought her home on their third and last date before her world turned upside down. Something happened between them that night, making it clear to her they could be more than friends. She lifted her gaze to his, mesmerized by the golden flecks in his eyes.

He leaned closer, their breaths tangling. She wanted him to kiss her. Her eyelids closed, anticipation of recapturing the kiss they'd shared all those years ago urging her to close the small gap between them.

The sound of a cough propelled Caitlyn back a few steps and her eyes flew open. Ian spun around to the doorway of the den. Granny and Emma were trying to sneak away.

Emma waved at them. "Sorry to interrupt y'all. We didn't mean to. Return to what you were doing."

They disappeared around the corner, but Granny could be heard saying, "You picked a great time to cough."

"Couldn't help it," Emma said in a disgruntled voice.

Caitlyn and Ian looked at each other and burst out laughing.

"We hear you," Granny shouted. "Y'all need to get some sleep. You don't want to be late tomorrow."

Caitlyn pressed her lips together at her grandmother's chiding.

"You mean today, Sally. It's one o'clock." The sound of a door closing followed Emma's last words.

Caitlyn's face burned with embarrassment. If they had kissed each other, she and Ian would never have heard the end of it.

He pivoted back to her. "They're right. I didn't realize it was so late." Moving nearer, he grazed a thumb across her cheek. He opened his mouth as if to say something, but instead he snapped it closed.

"Yeah, both of us will have a lot to do."

Ian switched off most of the lights throughout the house as they headed to the hallway with the bedrooms. As he strolled toward the end, his arm brushed against hers. His touch reminded her of their near kiss, and disappointment wove through her. She slowed her pace. This was the absolute worst time to be attracted to him. They both needed to focus on who had killed two women and was possibly trying to destroy her practice and her.

He stopped at the door to the room she and Granny were sharing. "Good night."

His intense look robbed her of a reply. She turned and reached for the doorknob of the guest room.

He clasped her left arm, swung her around toward him and tugged her against him. As he cupped her head, he kissed her with a gentle exploration that quickly intensified. When he finally pulled back, his hands still on her face, her legs grew weak.

He smiled. "Good night."

Caitlyn stepped away until her back flattened against the door. She couldn't think of anything to say.

"I've been wanting to do that again for seventeen years," he murmured.

To prevent throwing herself at him, she whirled, grasped the doorknob and hurried into the guest bedroom. She wasn't sure how she was going to get to sleep now, but she quickly got ready for bed in the dark and fumbled her way to the twin bed.

The touch of his mouth on hers stayed with her as she fell asleep, and the kiss was the first thing she thought about when she woke up the next morning as Granny shook her shoulder.

"Honey, breakfast is almost ready. It's seven."

"Thanks, Granny. I'll be there shortly." She had to concentrate on what she needed to do today rather than on what happened last night. Would he kiss her again? That question kept flitting in and out of her mind as she dressed in navy blue pants, a matching jacket and a white shirt. She hoped she presented a professional facade because right now she felt like her life was falling apart. After the past two days, she was afraid of what might happen today.

She left the bedroom and headed to the kitchen where Emma, Granny and Ian were already seated. Slicing a glance at Ian, she caught him looking at her. She hurried to the counter and poured coffee into a large to-go mug before taking the seat across from him.

"What are you two going to be doing today?" Caitlyn put strawberry jam on her piece of toast.

"Ian is coming back to get us at nine." Emma peered at her grandson. "We'll be at the church all day. With the deaths of Jane and Kelli, there'll be a lot to do."

"I wish I could help." Caitlyn scooped up a spoonful of scrambled eggs from a serving bowl.

Granny patted her hand on the table. "Honey, you have even more important work to do. You have to help Ian figure out who's killing your patients."

"Granny! You can't say anything to anyone about Kelli and Jane being my patients. It's not a secret, but I don't want y'all involved at all. Ian doesn't know what the motive is. The less said about the case the better."

"Ladies, I agree with Caitlyn. I want the community to be vigilant but not to go to any extreme measures that could lead to a tragedy."

Emma splayed her hand over her chest. "Oh my! We won't do that, Ian."

Granny harrumphed but kept her head down as though the most important thing she could do was eat her breakfast.

When Caitlyn finished her hasty meal, she pushed back her chair and rose. "I'd like to get to the office early to prepare for my first patient." She topped off her to-go mug with steaming, hot coffee that smelled wonderful. Right now, she could drink the whole pot following the restless night she'd had. She probably hadn't fallen asleep until five.

Once she'd gathered her notes and laptop from the

den, Caitlyn and Ian left. Outside she took a deep breath of air, laced with the scent of flowers. "At least it's going to be a beautiful day."

"I hope a whole lot better than the past two," Ian said as he settled into his SUV and started the engine. "The same police officer will be at your office this morning. I'll pick you up and take you to the station."

"Is this going to become our daily routine?"

"Consider me your chauffeur and bodyguard."

"I'm not used to being chauffeured around."

He slid her a smile that sent her heart beating faster. "But you're used to having a bodyguard?"

She chuckled. "No, thankfully." As the medical clinic came into view, she sobered. "And I don't want to get used to one. I want this case solved today."

"So do I. I don't want to think my brother could have a link to the case. I can't dismiss his link to Jane. Why was their relationship a secret?"

"Have you asked him?"

"No, but I will today. He's on my list of people to talk to this morning." Ian parked next to building, the lot already filling up. "When does the clinic open?"

"A few of the doctors start as early as seven. The day Jane was murdered I came in early for her appointment."

"Was she agitated about anything?"

"She was restless, prowling around a lot when she talked. I was seeing her because the doctor said her blood pressure had skyrocketed, likely from stress. She put undue pressure on herself, and she was trying to deal with not taking on all the problems of the world. Sometimes I think she just needed an outsider to listen to her."

"How long had she been a patient?"

"Seven months. The Shephard Foundation was expanding, and she didn't feel she was keeping up like she should. It was important to her and her father that she do a good job. She never once mentioned Sean in our sessions."

"Maybe the relationship wasn't that important to Jane."

"I hope Sean will answer your questions." As she climbed from the car, she prayed that Sean didn't have anything to do with Ian's case. She didn't have any siblings and had always appreciated Ian and Sean letting her tag along when she was young and they were at their grandmothers' houses.

"So do I." Ian headed for the main entrance, his gaze sweeping the terrain around them. "I wish there were cameras in the parking lot. I checked yesterday before picking you up. I wanted to view the footage."

"Believe me, I'm going to press for more than the ones at the front and back doors. It's sad that it's come to that, though."

He stepped to the side and signaled her to enter first. "But those cameras can be a big help for the police."

"I know. But Longhorn is losing its small-town feeling. Dallas is encroaching."

"That's what happens when you live near a big city."

Caitlyn strolled down the hallway to her office. "When will Officer Collins be here?"

"He should arrive in five or ten minutes. I won't leave until he comes."

"I didn't see my patient here yet." She glanced at her watch. "Of course, it's only seven forty. I was afraid if I stayed long at the table this morning, one of the grandmothers would say something about last night."

"About our almost-kiss in the den?"

She nodded and inserted her key into the door lock, his words bringing back all the feelings that had inundated her when he had finally kissed her in the hallway. Quickly, before she wanted to see if his kiss would have the same effect on her today, she turned the knob and pushed open the door of her office.

And found a chaotic mess of destruction before her.

SEVEN

Ian grabbed Caitlyn in midstep. "Don't. Stay here in the doorway. Let me check it out." Donning latex gloves, he withdrew his gun and slipped past her into the office.

Eyes wide, she nodded once.

Ian picked his way through all the trash, ripped-up papers and books, and smashed objects to the first of three other doors. The first one led to the private entrance for Caitlyn that opened onto another hallway. He peeked out into the empty short corridor. Next, he checked a closet, with a coat and sweater flung on the floor and items from storage boxes scattered a foot deep on them. The last door led into a small bathroom, surprisingly left untouched—except for *Stop me!* on the mirror over the sink, written in black. A capped marker lay in the basin. He picked it up and carefully dropped it into an evidence bag. Then he called both the sheriff and police chief about the break-in, since one body had been discovered outside Longhorn's town limits and the other within.

When he returned to the main office, he focused on Caitlyn rather than the destruction between them. She wasn't even aware he was looking at her. Her attention was fixed on her desk and the empty file cabinets behind it, with all the files strewn everywhere. She shook her head as though in shock and not believing what she was seeing.

"Caitlyn?"

Finally, their gazes embraced across the turmoil, tears pooling in her eyes. He quickly made his way across the room, cautious of where he stepped. When he stopped in front of her, she plastered herself against him, her whole body shaking. He embraced her, wishing he could take all this away.

"Why would someone do this?"

"It's the work of the killer. He left his message on the mirror in the bathroom."

A shudder rippled down her. "You're right he doesn't want me to stop him—he wants to scare me and kill me."

"I'm not going to let him do that. You'll be guarded at all times."

She leaned back, her arms loosely locked around his. "I'm canceling my appointments until this is resolved. I can't put my patients in any more danger than they already are just because I'm their therapist. I went into this field to help others, and instead I'm hurting people."

He laid his fingers over her mouth. "Don't say that, and don't think it. He's the only one responsible for what's happening." A tear ran down her cheek, and he swept it away. "I've called the sheriff and police chief, and they are on their way. I want this place processed."

"What if he stole some of my files? He broke into my locked cabinets, possibly looking for certain people. I'll have to go through all of this too."

"I agree. We need to know what was stolen, if anything." He stepped back and clasped both of her hands. "After Officer Collins arrives, is there a place you can go, until we're finished going through your office? Collins will be with you."

"There's a break room down the hall at the end." She pointed to the right, then patted the strap of the bag she had her laptop in. "I'm glad he didn't get my computer."

When Blake Collins came around the corner, Ian motioned him to join them. The policeman slowed as he passed the open doorway into the office. "I need you to sit with Caitlyn while we go through the crime scene."

"Chief Franklin called me and filled me in."

"We're going to camp out in the break room, Officer Collins." Caitlyn started down the corridor.

Ian watched until she and the policeman disappeared inside the room before he moved to the entrance of the office, scanning the disarray. This would take hours to go through. He entered and began taking pictures on his right side, homing in on certain areas, especially the ones involving the files. Maybe in all this mess there would be a piece of evidence to help him narrow down who the murderer was. The more he photographed different sections, the more he realized the anger behind this destruction, the power behind tearing some files in half. Were those people significant in some way to the killer? He hoped Caitlyn could answer that.

After lunch, Caitlyn sat on the floor in her office with stacks of papers surrounding her as she tried to put her files back together. She felt as if she were in the middle of a sea with no sight of land anywhere on the horizon.

"This is the last of your papers." Ian placed them on the smallest pile. "Are you sure I can't help you?"

"No. I'm the only one who can do this. The records are confidential."

"I won't read anything beyond the name."

She smiled up at him. "I know, but even that I need to keep private. My patients' privacy has already been compromised with this break-in. But thanks for all the work you've done so far on this room." She glanced around, the left side of the office beginning to look normal. "I'm using this time to jot down notes from different files that I want to study and go over in-depth later concerning your case. This actually isn't a total loss of time."

Ian knelt next to her and placed his hands on her shoulders. "When you're through I'll massage your shoulders again."

"I imagine my muscles have hardened into rocks."

"Yep, definitely stiff." His gaze met hers. "Officer Collins will be back shortly. I won't be gone long, but I have to interview a couple of people."

"Who?"

"Employees at the grocery store where Kelli Williams worked. And Sean about Jane."

"Do you want me to come with you to talk to Sean?"

"No." He gestured to the stacks around her. "This is more important. With this break-in, I'm even more convinced you're the key to solving the case."

"That's what has me worried because I have no idea why."

He rubbed two fingers across her forehead as though he could wipe away her worry. "I know, and I wish I could take that away from you."

"And I'm the one who tells her patients not to worry unless you can do something about it. That it's a wasted activity that hurts your body." She leaned toward him and whispered, "Don't tell any of them that I'm worried. There's only so much I can do. The rest is out of my control, and even with all my training, I can't stop the fear wanting to take over."

His solemn expression underscored his similar feelings. "It's not easy to do. Pray. The Lord will help you."

"Thanks. I needed that reminder."

Ian rose. "Officer Collins is here. I'm only a phone call away."

The moment Ian left, an emptiness filled Caitlyn. When he was around she felt safe, just as she used to before she was raped by a guy she'd dated off and on in high school. Byron Woods had shattered her trust in people, and it took her years to piece it back together. And now this. Deep down she knew the killer was someone in her life.

After Ian left, Officer Collins said from the doorway, "Do you want me to help with the cleanup?"

"No, but thanks for asking. Most of this I have to see to."

Ian helping was one thing but anyone else, even a police officer, was an invasion of privacy. She spent more time here than she did at her town house. Her work was important to her. When this case was solved, she hoped she'd have a practice left. All she ever wanted to do was help others who were in pain, like she had been at eighteen. She should have brought charges against Byron, but she'd been so broken and afraid that all she'd wanted to do was hide. Now she didn't know where Byron was. Had he ever raped another woman? That question still haunted her, especially whenever she counseled a rape victim.

"Ma'am, there's someone in the hallway who wants to talk to you." Officer Collins stood at the threshold, blocking Rob Owens, the nurse.

"Is there something wrong, Rob?"

When the policeman moved to the side, Rob came a few feet into the room. "Claire thought if any of us had some downtime with patients, we should see if you needed help."

"Thanks for volunteering, but I'm fine. Tell Claire this is something I have to do." Caitlyn started to look away, but Rob didn't move to leave. "Is there something else?"

"As you know, I'm always one of the first ones here in the morning. This morning I came in even earlier because I had some chart work to finish. When I slowed to turn into the parking lot, a black truck sped out of it, almost hitting me. It doesn't belong to anyone on staff."

"Did you see who was driving it?"

"The windows were so dark I couldn't see the driver. It happened fast. I didn't even think to get a license plate number until it was too late."

"Let the officer know all the details you can remember."

"I will."

Once the nurse stepped out into the corridor, Caitlyn went back to work. The people she worked with were supportive. All morning they had stopped by the break room to tell her how sorry they were about the robbery. Since she'd been sitting here and reassembling the files, so far she hadn't found anything stolen. Most of the files had some of their contents already back in them.

A couple were completed. Once she had all her notes in the right places, she would take the folders to Emma's, read through them and put all the pages back in order.

She checked her watch and wondered if Ian was at the Pierce ranch yet. Would Sean be there? Would he talk to Ian?

Alice opened the door to Ian. "Sean's in his office. He's been there all day. He even ate his lunch at his desk."

"How is he?"

"Quiet. Solemn."

"Did he know about Kelli's car being found on the lake side of our property?"

"Yes. The sheriff stopped by and talked to him yesterday evening. He came back this morning and was with Sean in his office for half an hour."

He did? Tom hadn't said anything to him about it. Of course, this was the sheriff's investigation, and he was only assisting him. He understood why Tom needed to deal with Sean, but did the sheriff think Sean was connected? In his gut, he didn't think his older brother would have killed Jane and Kelli.

"Thanks, Alice." Ian headed for the back of the house.

At the door to the office, he thought about knocking but, for some reason, he decided not to. He gripped the knob, turned it and swung the door open.

To find his brother with a handgun pointed at his temple.

Sean's eyes fixed on him. "Leave me alone."

"I'm not going to. Put the gun down, Sean. Killing yourself isn't the answer to any problem."

The hand holding the weapon shook as though he was battling within himself to pull the trigger or put the gun down. "Please, Sean. I love you. I don't want to lose you too." With each word he spoke, he took a step closer to his sibling.

"If you don't stop, I'll shoot myself, and it'll be your fault."

"No, it won't." He wouldn't let his brother blame him for what was happening to him. "You are in control."

"Control? No, I'm not. People I care about are dying." His eyes shone. "First Mom, then Dad and now Jane. At least I didn't find Jane—" tears streamed down his face "—dead."

"You didn't find Dad dead. He died in the hospital."

"But I found him passed out in his office. He never woke up. He died three hours later. I couldn't save Mom or Dad. Jane and I had been together the night before. We had a great time."

"Why did you keep your relationship a secret?" Ian wanted to move even closer, but getting Sean to open up might help talk himself out of pulling the trigger.

"Because our fathers didn't get along, especially for the past ten years when you were rarely here to see. As you know, we've a long-standing issue over the property line on the western side that involves the creek that feeds into the lake. When Dad died, I tried to settle the dispute, but Jack Shephard never had the time to sit down and discuss it." Sean lowered the gun from his head, but he still held it. "Jane didn't want her father to ruin what we were starting to feel for each other. But I hated the secrecy. I haven't been handling it well."

"When did you start drinking?"

"After Dad died. I miss him so much. I don't know…"

Sean dropped his head and stared at his hand holding the gun. "I'm all alone now."

Ian had learned how to be alone—Sean hadn't. His back tensed, Ian sidled toward the chair in front of the desk and eased down onto it. "No, you aren't. You have me and Nana. She's worried about you. Also Alice. What you want to do isn't the answer."

Sean released a long breath. "Jane had been seeing Caitlyn. She was helping her deal with her domineering father and the pressure she felt."

Ian didn't smell any alcohol, but he risked asking anyway. "When was the last time you had a drink?"

"I haven't taken a drink in thirty-six hours. I don't like what it does to me."

"Caitlyn would help you. She was really worried about you the other night." Ian leaned forward, laying his palm out flat. "Give me the gun. I'm not leaving until you do."

Lifting his head, Sean released his grip on the weapon and pushed it toward Ian.

"I'll call Caitlyn. Do you want to see her today?" Ian asked.

Sean nodded.

"I'd like to suggest you come to Nana's house. She and Sally could use you during the day to help them and make sure nothing happens to them."

"Why are they in danger?" Confusion clouded his brother's dark eyes.

"Have you been following the news the past several days?"

"No. I couldn't deal with hearing about Jane's death. It was bad enough when I saw her car on fire yesterday."

Sean had never been a good actor, able to hide his

true feelings from others for long. Ian didn't think his brother had anything to do with the deaths of Jane or Kelli. He gave Sean a rundown on what had happened.

"Kelli Williams from church?"

"Yes. Her car was found on our property near the lake, not far from where Jane's car was set on fire."

His eyes round, Sean straightened. "I've really not been paying attention to what's been going on. There were days after Dad died, I didn't want to get out of bed. Jane changed that, at least. She became my reason to leave my bedroom, the ranch. She used to ride along the lake as I did. We started meeting each other to ride together." As his brother talked about Jane, his voice softened.

He couldn't leave Sean alone at the ranch. He didn't want to make his brother go to a hospital because that would only create a worse situation. "Caitlyn and her grandmother are staying with Nana and me because the killer has been contacting Caitlyn. He says he wants her to stop him, but I don't think that's really what it is. Her house and office have been broken into."

"You think she's in danger."

Although not a question, Ian said, "Yes. Somehow she is tied to him, but so far we haven't been able to connect who it is or the reason behind the murders."

"I can't leave Alice here alone. Do you think Nana would mind if she came?"

"She wouldn't. Alice and Nana are good friends. You and I can camp out in the den, and Alice can have my bedroom." This way Sean would have support and help nearby. "Let's get what you want to take with you and then speak with Alice. After you're settled, I need to pick Caitlyn up at her office."

Still grasping the gun, Ian followed Sean to his room but stayed in the hallway while he withdrew his cell phone to let his grandmother and Caitlyn know what was going on. He'd known Sean was in a dark place, but he hadn't realized how bad it was. In the middle of this investigation, he had to keep his brother safe and alive too.

Caitlyn finished boxing up her files, labeling the outside of the carton with the year the patient had started with her. She was eager to return to Emma's house. Sean needed help and had finally agreed to talk with her. She told Ian that if she felt his brother needed more intense assistance, she would recommend a treatment center not far from Longhorn. It wasn't technically a hospital, but she worried Sean might look at it as if it were. Besides going through her patient folders, she would have something to do while she took the next week off. Most of her clients had been informed. Several patients were relieved she wouldn't be in the office next week because of what was going on with the double murders that had rocked Longhorn. But a few were very upset with her, especially Charles Thorne and Paul Nichols.

She agreed to meet with both men at their houses to have their sessions. She still needed to tell Ian that, and she hoped he wouldn't disapprove. Maybe it wouldn't be an issue if the killer was arrested by then. Each of the men's appointments was toward the end of the following week.

Ian appeared in the doorway of her office. "Are you ready?"

She glanced around to make sure she had everything she would need at Emma's. "Yes. I asked Rob

"4 for 4" MINI-SURVEY

We are prepared to **REWARD** you with 2 FREE books and 2 FREE gifts for completing our MINI SURVEY!

FREE
Value Over
$20!

You'll get...

TWO FREE BOOKS & TWO FREE GIFTS

ust for participating in our Mini Survey!

Dear Reader,

IT'S A FACT: if you answer 4 quick questions, we'll send you 4 FREE REWARDS!

I'm not kidding you. As a leading publisher of women's fiction, we value your opinions... and your time. That's why we are prepared to **reward** you handsomely for completing our mini-survey. In fact, we have 4 Free Rewards for you, including 2 free books and 2 free gifts.

As you may have guessed, that's why our mini-survey is called **"4 for 4".** Answer 4 questions and get 4 Free Rewards. It's that simple!

Thank you for participating in our survey,

Pam Powers

www.ReaderService.com

To get your 4 FREE REWARDS:
Complete the survey below and return the insert today to receive 2 FREE BOOKS and 2 FREE GIFTS guaranteed!

▼ DETACH AND MAIL CARD TODAY! ▼

"4 for 4" MINI-SURVEY

1 Is reading one of your favorite hobbies?
☐ YES ☐ NO

2 Do you prefer to read instead of watch TV?
☐ YES ☐ NO

3 Do you read newspapers and magazines?
☐ YES ☐ NO

4 Do you enjoy trying new book series with FREE BOOKS?
☐ YES ☐ NO

YES! I have completed the above Mini-Survey. Please send me my 4 FREE REWARDS (worth over $20 retail). I understand that I am under no obligation to buy anything, as explained on the back of this card.

❏ I prefer the regular-print edition
153/353 IDL GMYM

❏ I prefer the larger-print edition
107/307 IDL GMYM

FIRST NAME   LAST NAME

ADDRESS

APT.#   CITY

STATE/PROV.   ZIP/POSTAL CODE

Offer limited to one per household and not applicable to series that subscriber is currently receiving. **Your Privacy**—The Reader Service is committed to protecting your privacy. Our Privacy Policy is available online at www.ReaderService.com or upon request from the Reader Service. We make a portion of our mailing list available to reputable third parties that offer products we believe may interest you. If you prefer that we not exchange your name with third parties, or if you wish to clarify or modify your communication preferences, please visit us at www.ReaderService.com/consumerschoice or write to us at Reader Service Preference Service, P.O. Box 9062, Buffalo, NY 14240-9062. Include your complete name and address.   SLI-218-MS17

© 2017 HARLEQUIN ENTERPRISES LIMITED ® and ™ are trademarks owned and used by the trademark owner and/or its licensee. Printed in the U.S.A.

READER SERVICE—Here's how it works:

Accepting your 2 free Love Inspired® Suspense books and 2 free gifts (gifts valued at approximately $10.00 retail) places you under no obligation to buy anything. You may keep the books and gifts and return the shipping statement marked "cancel." If you do not cancel, about a month later we'll send you 6 additional books and bill you just $5.24 each for the regular-print edition or $5.74 each for the larger-print edition in the U.S. or $5.74 each for the regular-print edition or $6.24 each for the larger-print edition in Canada. That is a savings of at least 13% off the cover price. It's quite a bargain! Shipping and handling is just 50¢ per book in the U.S. and 75¢ per book in Canada*. You may cancel at any time, but if you choose to continue, every month we'll send you 6 more books, which you may either purchase at the discount price plus shipping and handling or return to us and cancel your subscription. *Terms and prices subject to change without notice. Prices do not include applicable taxes. Sales tax applicable in N.Y. Canadian residents will be charged applicable taxes. Offer not valid in Quebec. Books received may not be as shown. All orders subject to approval. Credit or debit balances in a customer's account(s) may be offset by any other outstanding balance owed by or to the customer. Please allow 4 to 6 weeks for delivery. Offer available while quantities last.

BUSINESS REPLY MAIL
FIRST-CLASS MAIL   PERMIT NO. 717   BUFFALO, NY

POSTAGE WILL BE PAID BY ADDRESSEE

READER SERVICE
PO BOX 1341
BUFFALO NY 14240-8571

NO POSTAGE
NECESSARY
IF MAILED
IN THE
UNITED STATES

◄ If offer card is missing write to: Reader Service, P.O. Box 1341, Buffalo, NY 14240-8531 or visit www.ReaderService.com ◄

Owens and Blake to help us take the boxes to your SUV. With them helping, we'll only need to make two trips." She covered the space between them. "Where did Blake go?"

"He didn't leave. He'll be back soon."

"I'll let Rob know I'm ready to leave." She made a quick call to the nurse. "How's Sean doing at your grandmother's?"

Ian chuckled. "The second we arrived, he had three ladies doting on him. With Alice, Sally and Nana, my brother won't get much alone time."

"Poor guy, but he needs to know there are a lot of people who care about him."

Rob poked his head in. "I'm ready. I was getting ready to leave, so perfect timing. Where are the boxes I need to help you with?"

Caitlyn pointed to the three stacks.

"Are you moving out?" Rob headed in the direction she'd indicated.

"No, but I'm going to work from home next week."

He squatted and lifted two cartons. "You aren't meeting patients here?"

"No. I need some time away. This break-in was a good excuse to do that," she said, while Blake returned and grabbed a load too.

With their help, the back of Ian's SUV was filled up with evidence of her seven years of practice.

"Thanks, Blake and Rob, for helping me."

"Anytime." Rob dug his keys out of his pocket and walked to his car.

Exhaustion wove through her. She shouldn't have stopped. Now all she wanted to do was sleep. Caitlyn climbed into Ian's vehicle while he shook hands with

Blake, who then also left. She leaned against the head-rest and closed her eyes.

When the driver's-side door opened and closed, she rolled her head focus to on Ian. "You look as tired as I am. I don't know how sharp I'm going to be checking these files tonight. Over the years, I've had some patients with problems that break my heart. I have to be objective, but there were times that was hard. I've had a few I couldn't help. One moved away. Another stopped coming, even when I told him I would adjust the cost of a session to fit his budget. The worst was six months ago. I had a young man who committed suicide. It devastated me. He'd been making progress, then he missed a session. He'd called the receptionist to cancel. When I called him to see if everything was okay, he didn't answer." Her throat tightened at the memory.

"How did you find out he committed suicide?"

"Later he called me back. He told me he couldn't live any longer. I stayed on the phone with him while I drove to his apartment. But by the time I arrived at his place, the medication he had used to overdose on had killed him. He left a note, saying he couldn't handle life anymore." *Why didn't I see it?* "During his last session with me, there were no signs he was thinking about suicide." But still, she had questioned herself concerning her plan of treatment for him.

"We both have difficult jobs. I try to remain objective in a case, but sometimes it isn't easy, especially when there's a child involved."

"For a while I contemplated working with children but, in the end, I knew I couldn't do it for that very reason. I'd never be able to stay detached."

"You were always so good with kids. Didn't you

take care of the nursery at church every Sunday as a teenager?"

"I still do, once a month. I love holding the babies." When she'd learned she was pregnant from the rape, she'd decided to keep the child. She'd begun to think being a mother was the blessing from the life-changing ordeal. But she'd miscarried when she was six months along, and that devastated her life all over again. She knew she was going to have a girl and had already named her Kathleen. Byron might have taken her innocence from her, but her baby was hers to love as though nothing tragic had caused her conception.

"Then why aren't you married with several of your own babies? You would be a great mother."

She'd visualized that herself with Kathleen. Byron had robbed her of a sense of self-assurance, and even now she grappled with being confident in certain situations with men. And for that reason, she'd rarely dated and instead threw her life into her studies and later her career. "I never found the right man. How about you?"

When Ian didn't say anything for a moment, she glanced at his profile, the line of his jaw hard, as if he were gritting his teeth. Had she touched on a forbidden subject? "You don't have to answer that."

Ian pulled into his grandmother's driveway and switched off the engine. "I was engaged once."

His statement surprised her. "Emma never told me that."

"It's because I wasn't engaged for very long. I hadn't told my family yet."

"What happened?" she asked, knowing from his stiff posture and tight hold on the steering wheel that she was treading into a subject he didn't like to discuss.

"Are you asking as a therapist or friend?"

"Which one do you need?"

He released his grip on the wheel and opened his door. "We'd better get inside before the grandmothers get overly curious. Nana is getting quite good at interrogating me."

In other words, he didn't want to share why he'd never got married. She understood. She had her own secrets, which were best left in the past.

As she strolled to the porch, the front door swung open, and Granny filled the entrance with her lips pinched together. "Are we late for dinner?" Caitlyn whispered to Ian next to her.

"I don't think so, but then I don't know when dinner is supposed to be. Nana hasn't had the evening meal at the same time the whole week I've been here."

"What's wrong, Granny?"

"I just got a call from the killer."

EIGHT

As Sally stepped to the side, Ian hurried Caitlyn into the house. "What did the man say?"

Caitlyn's grandmother opened her mouth, then snapped it close. "Shh. I don't want the others to hear. Emma is barely holding herself together. She hates having to stay in the house all the time." She took Caitlyn's arm and pulled her down the hall, through the kitchen to the back door and out onto the patio. She gestured toward the four-foot fence that enclosed the yard. "We should be safe, especially with the police involvement and protection." When she turned, she faced away from the home. "You two had just parked in the driveway when I received a call on my cell phone. When I said hello, silence was all there was. Then when I was going to hang up, an odd, husky voice said, 'Tell Caitlyn to stop me.' Didn't the killer write *Stop me!* on Jane's photo? And he called her radio show too and said that."

"Yes, but you still need to keep quiet about that. The town is already panicked enough." Ian pivoted to mentally pan the backyard. "Let's go back inside and get your phone. I want to see what number he used. We still haven't found Kelli's, but we've put a trace on it."

"I was in my bedroom. I left it on the dresser when I saw you two pull up. I'll go get it." Sally scurried ahead of Ian and Caitlyn into the house.

"Where's Alice, Emma and Sean?" Ian asked before Sally disappeared into the hallway.

"In the den, trying to figure out where you and Sean will sleep."

"We'll sleep on the floor," Ian said to the departing Sally, then turned to Caitlyn. "I hope Sean isn't shutting down. I hated leaving him with three ladies who love to dote."

"Let's go rescue him. I need to talk to him. I thought I might before dinner."

"That sounds good."

In the hall near the den, Caitlyn stopped Ian's progress and pulled him around to face her. "You know I can't tell you what he says to me unless Sean is okay with that."

"Don't ask him to. Right now, I just want him to get help. I'm hoping that he'll tell me what's going on on his own."

She smiled at him and slipped her hand off his arm. "I hope so too."

When Ian entered the den, Sean sat between Alice and Emma, who were conversing about how to put some cushions together for Sean and Ian. The wide-eyed look that Sean shot Ian screamed his brother's need of rescue.

"Emma, you have a king-size bed. Can Alice or Granny share your bed while the other stays with me? That way Sean and Ian can stay in the third bedroom." Caitlyn looked from the women to Sean, then Ian. "Wouldn't that work, rather than try to make beds on the hard floor?"

"Well, yes, that'll work." Emma rose from the sofa. "I'm glad that's been taken care of. Alice, thanks for offering to help me with dinner. We'd better start now."

Alice and Emma headed for the kitchen.

Sean relaxed against the back cushion. "Thanks for thinking of that, Caitlyn."

"Are you okay, Sean? You looked like you felt cornered." Caitlyn made her way to the couch and eased down onto the other end from Sean.

"I was! I've been refereeing since Ian left me alone with the ladies."

"Welcome to my world," Ian said with a chuckle. He glanced from his brother to Caitlyn. "I need to see Sally. Will you two behave while I'm gone?"

"Of course." Caitlyn shifted her attention to Sean. "I'd like to talk to you. Is that all right?"

Ian's brother nodded.

"I'll let y'all know when dinner is ready." Ian walked toward the hallway and shut the door as he left.

He went in search of Sally, relieved that Sean hadn't said no to talking to Caitlyn. He wanted his brother back. What was happening in Longhorn was tearing the town apart. He didn't want Sean to be an emotional victim.

Ian found Caitlyn's grandmother coming out of her bedroom with her cell phone in her hand. She gave it to him, the screen showing the information of the last caller. "It's not Kelli Williams's number. Can I take this?"

"Sure. I have my calls from my home number transferred to this one. Not many people know my cell number. When will I get it back?"

"A few hours at most. Can I borrow your house key?"

Sally blinked rapidly. "Why?"

"I want to check your house."

"You think the killer is in my house?"

"I don't know. Stay here and help Alice and Nana in the kitchen. Caitlyn is talking with Sean in the den. I'll feel better if I do a walk-through of your house."

"Because the killer is fixated on Caitlyn?"

"It's a precaution. That's all." After today, there was no doubt the guy had a reason to involve Caitlyn. If he could figure out why, then he might find the killer— hopefully before someone else died.

Ian left Nana's house and crossed the yard to Sally's. When he unlocked the front door and stepped inside the home, the eerie quiet churned his gut. Chills tingled down his spine. Everything looked in order, but he didn't have a good feeling. He remembered Caitlyn's town house had been in perfect order except for the photo pinned to the door. He glanced over his shoulder and sighed in relief when he didn't see a photo anywhere.

Weapon drawn, Ian walked through the living and dining rooms, everything again seemingly in order. He stepped into the kitchen, recalling only a few days ago he and Caitlyn had eaten lunch together there. After being at Jane's dump site earlier that day, the sight of Caitlyn had lifted his spirits.

As he proceeded, he dug into his pocket for his cell phone to call the sheriff and let him know about the killer contacting Sally and the number he'd called from. He hoped Tom could trace it. While he headed down the hallway to check the rest of the house, he punched Tom's phone number in. As it rang, he entered Sally's bedroom, his attention glued to a photo lying on a pillow.

"Hello. I hope you have good news for me," Tom said.

Ian held the phone to his ear while juggling the grip on his gun. "I'm at Sally Rhodes's house and…"

Something heavy struck the back of his head. Pain flashed through him. His gun flew out of his hand. He started to turn to defend himself when an object smashed into the side of his face.

And everything went dark.

Caitlyn exchanged a few pleasantries with Sean, his tensed posture relaxing. "Tell me what led to you picking up the gun and pointing it at yourself today."

Sean blinked rapidly, sitting straight up. "You don't pull any punches."

"And in the past, you never did either. We've been friends for years. I'm concerned about you. I want to understand your reasons and the feelings you had at the time."

"I'd just returned from the Shephards' house. Jack took one look at me and began yelling that his baby was dead because of me."

"Why did he say that?"

"Because the morning of her death Jane had told him she was dating me. He had said to Jane he would do anything to keep us apart. It's not a secret that Jack and my dad had issues over the border of our ranches."

"Why were you drinking that day?"

"I knew how Jane felt about her father. She'd been sure she could convince him that I was perfect for her and that it was time the feud over our ranches be resolved. If we married, then the ranches could be merged into one. Jane did everything her dad asked. She adored him and feared him."

Exactly the impression Caitlyn had come to over the months she'd been counseling Jane. The young woman never said anything about Sean, but Caitlyn had sensed she was seeing someone important to her. Could the senator, in his rage, kill his own daughter? He could have killed Jane, then left for Austin. He hadn't wanted Caitlyn to talk to Ian about Jane's sessions. It was Mrs. Shephard who'd given her permission. But what about Kelli's murder? How would that connect to Jane's?

"I don't think you're the killer, but do you blame yourself in any way for Jane's death?"

Sean's shoulders sagged, and he lowered his head. "I should have been able to protect her somehow. Instead I went home after seeing Jane and drank more and more when I couldn't get hold of her by phone. I figured Jack had convinced her to stay away from me. I tried to tell her he wouldn't come around. He was stubborn and ruthless at times. I would have been satisfied if we just met in secret. I would…"

"Would what?"

Shaking his head, he folded his arms over his chest, avoiding eye contact.

He was closing himself off. "Do you want to find Jane's killer?" she asked.

He lifted his head, and his sharp gaze fixed on her. "Yes."

Good. He had a reason to live. He still had more to share and work through. He'd lost two people he loved within months of each other and was struggling to deal with their deaths. "Then you need to help Ian. Think about your conversations with Jane. Did anyone stalk or bother her? Did she complain about anyone?"

The den door slammed open. Granny, as white as the

shirt she wore, rushed into the room. "There are two police cars in my driveway and I can't find Ian. He was going to check my house."

Sean and Caitlyn simultaneously jumped to their feet. While Sean exited the den first, Caitlyn stopped to say, "You, Alice and Emma stay on the front porch. Do not follow us. I'll let you know what happened." Then she hurried outside after Sean as another cruiser pulled up and the police chief climbed from it.

Not a good sign. Had Ian found something? Then she heard a siren, its sound growing closer as the seconds ticked. An ambulance? Her heartbeat thundered against her skull, drowning out the noise slightly. A police officer stopped Sean a few feet from the porch.

"What's going on in there?" Sean asked, his hands opening and closing at his sides.

"I'm not at liberty—"

"My brother's in there."

Caitlyn touched Sean's arm. "Blake, I'm so glad you're here. What's happening?" She gestured toward Granny standing between Alice and Emma. "This is my grandmother's house and she's beside herself. Ian came over to check on the place. Is he all right?"

"Ma'am, I'm not—"

The arrival of an ambulance coming down the street interrupted Officer Collins's explanation.

Caitlyn swung her attention from the vehicle parking at the curb to Blake. "How bad is he?"

"I don't know."

Sean stepped into the policeman's personal space. "You can't send my brother to the hospital. He'll die there."

While Blake was distracted, Caitlyn ran up the stairs

to the porch, reaching for the door. Before she could grasp the handle, Chief Franklin came out, his expression grim. "Is Ian all right?" she asked in a breathless voice.

"He will be." He moved Caitlyn and himself to the side to allow the EMTs inside.

When Sean spied the police chief, he skirted Blake Collins and took the steps two at a time. "What happened?"

"Ian was attacked and knocked out."

"Is he conscious?"

The police chief looked at Caitlyn. "Yes."

"Coherent?"

"Yes."

"Can Sean and I see him? His grandmother will want to know how he is. I'd like to say I talked with him."

Chief Franklin nodded. "But not until he comes out here. This is a crime scene and will need to be processed. The killer has been in your grandmother's house."

Caitlyn turned to Sean. "Will you please escort Emma over here so she can see for herself Ian will be okay?" When he left and she and the police chief were alone on the porch, Caitlyn asked, "How do you know?"

"A photo with the words *Stop me!* was left on a pillow in a bedroom. It appears to be your grandmother's room."

"Who's the victim?"

"I don't know."

"Can I see if it's one of my patients?" She prayed it wasn't.

Chief Franklin watched Sean bringing Emma across the yard. "Later. I don't want others to see it."

At that moment, a paramedic pushed against the screen door as he guided the gurney out of Granny's place. Caitlyn hurried to Ian, a white bandage around his head. His gaze flicked to hers, and the pain she saw in his eyes tested her resolve to stay strong. All she wanted to do was hold him.

Give him the comfort he has given me. Please, Lord, heal Ian and help us find the killer. Neither one of us will rest until the guy is brought to justice.

The EMTs stopped at the top of the porch steps while Emma mounted them with Sean behind her.

His grandmother's eyes filled with tears. She touched his chest. "Sean and I will be at the hospital. I'll take care of you." She leaned down and kissed his cheek, then pivoted around to Sean.

He hugged her. "Don't worry about the ladies. I'll take care of them." Then in order for the paramedics to take the gurney down to the sidewalk, Sean led Emma down the stairs so they could get out of the way.

Ian's attention swiveled to Caitlyn. "I'm okay. Have a police officer take you to the hospital. Sean will need you."

She took his hand and held it between hers. "I'll take care of your family. I know how your brother feels about hospitals."

Chief Franklin clasped her arm and urged her away from the gurney. "I'll take her, Ian."

"Thanks," Ian murmured, then closed his eyes as the paramedics maneuvered him down the steps.

Caitlyn stared at them leaving. "His wound is bleeding through the bandage."

"Head injuries can bleed a lot. He's tough."

She slanted a look at Chief Franklin. "I want to see

the photo before we go to the hospital. This killer has got to be caught."

He scanned the area. "Let's go to my car. I don't want anyone in the gathering crowd to see the picture." As the police chief escorted her toward his SUV, several neighbors approached.

"Chief, what's going on?" a lady who lived across the street asked.

A man Caitlyn recognized from the newsroom at the station stepped in front of the group forming around her and the police chief. "Does this have anything to do with the 'Stop me' killer?"

"No comment at this time." Chief Franklin took hold of Caitlyn's upper arm and navigated a path for them through the people.

When she settled in the passenger seat in his vehicle, his cell phone rang. She stared out the side window while he spoke with the sheriff. Could the killer be watching or in the crowd? She took out her cell phone and took several photos of the throng to show Ian.

The picture of him lying on the gurney popped into her mind. Head wounds could be serious. In a short time, he'd become important in her life again. He was trying to solve the case and keep her safe, but what she was feeling for him was more than gratitude. It was wrapped up in emotions that she'd buried many years ago when she'd left in the summer she was eighteen.

Once Chief Franklin finished his call, Caitlyn swung her gaze from watching Sean escort Emma, Granny and Alice to Ian's SUV to the police chief. "That reporter said the 'Stop me' killer. When did that start?"

"That's the first I heard it. We've played down what the killer has been writing."

"Maybe he heard about that call on my show." Caitlyn focused on the ambulance pulling away from the curb. "Do you know how the killer got into my grandmother's house?"

"No. The doors and windows were closed and locked."

"Someone had a key?"

"That's definitely a possibility."

"The same as my office." The realization the killer could be someone close to her robbed her of breath for a long moment. Her lungs burned, and she finally inhaled. In a panic, she searched for her purse for a few seconds until she remembered it was still in the den. "How? I have only two sets of keys. One in my purse and the other…"

"Where?"

"In my locked desk at my office."

"Which was broken into this morning. Were they there when you were cleaning up?"

She closed her eyes and tried to remember what she'd found when she put her desk items back in place. Mentally she was back in her trashed office, sitting at her desk putting the notepads, pens and pencils back in the drawer. Her hand brushed against her set of keys. "Yes, they were in the very back. Everything else had been thrown on the floor."

"But not the keys. Interesting." The police chief started his car and drove away from Granny's house.

"Why do you say that?"

"If the keys were the only item left in your drawers, I guess he could have overlooked them, but I don't think so, since that seemed the way he got into your office."

"So, it's someone who could somehow get access to my keys either in my purse or office."

"They could have made an impression of them and had your keys duplicated."

She was the prey. She had to figure out who the killer was before he did it again.

At a stoplight, Chief Franklin passed her a clear evidence bag with a photo in it. "Do you know who this is?"

As she stared at the young woman posed like the others, her heart felt as though it had sunk into her stomach. "Yes. It's one of my patients. Missy Quinn. I just saw her yesterday. She and her husband moved here five months ago from Dallas. They'd wanted a quieter, safer community." Her gut roiled at the irony of that.

"Do you know her address?"

"Not off the top of my head, but the receptionist at the clinic should still be there, and she could pull it up for me." Caitlyn called and jotted down the information the receptionist gave her on Missy Quinn, and Caitlyn gave it to the chief.

"Have you met her husband?"

"No."

"Do you mind if we take a short detour to see if her husband is home? I promise I'll get you to the medical center right after that."

Caitlyn glanced at her watch. It'd only been a few minutes since they had left Granny's house. "That's fine. I'll call my grandmother and let her know we'll be late, but if there is any bad news concerning Ian, she should call me."

As Chief Franklin made a U-turn and headed for the Quinns' house, Caitlyn got ahold of her grandmother and told her she would be there a little late. "How's Ian? Have you heard anything?" she asked to keep Granny from trying to find out what she was doing. She couldn't tell anyone but Ian who the victim was until the family was notified.

"The doctor is checking him out right now. I can't believe the killer was in my house. I don't know if I want to live there anymore."

"Just make sure Officer Collins and Sean stay with you, Emma and Alice. I'll be there soon." Caitlyn disconnected the call as the chief pulled up to the Quinns' home.

The neatly trimmed yard with splashes of floral color everywhere was the same as that time she'd visited Missy at her house—perfect. According to what Missy had told her, she didn't work outside the home but spent a lot of time in her yard when the weather permitted. Caitlyn fought the grief threatening to overwhelm her. She had to remain focused on the case if she wanted to help them solve the murders.

When Chief Franklin rang the doorbell, no one came to answer it. After pressing it again and waiting another few minutes, he tried to peek inside the front window but the curtains were drawn. "I'll have to come back later. Do you know where Missy's husband works?"

"In Dallas, somewhere. I don't know a lot about him. They've been married a couple of years and have moved around a few times."

"I'll have an officer drive by occasionally to see when he comes home. If there's a wreck on the highway, the Dallas commute can be a lot longer."

"Yes, I've been stuck in it before."

"Who hasn't!" Chief Franklin opened the passenger door. "Let's get to the Longhorn Medical Center."

As he pulled away from the house, Caitlyn looked at the home Missy had made so inviting and cheerful. When Caitlyn turned away to look ahead, for a split second she thought she saw the curtain in the large picture window move. She swiveled back around, but everything seemed in place. Was Missy's husband or someone else in the house? Or was she imagining things? She was so tired it seemed anything was possible.

NINE

As Sean pulled the SUV up to the covered exit at the medical center, Ian sat in the wheelchair with Caitlyn standing next to him, her hand on his shoulder. His head pounded despite the medication he'd taken. But this hadn't been the only injury and stitches he'd gotten during his career in law enforcement. He would work through the pain and find the killer.

"Who's with Sally and Nana?" he asked after settling onto the back seat.

Caitlyn slipped into the front. "Chief Franklin has assigned an officer to Emma's house whether you're there or not."

"Good. Because I don't intend to sit at Nana's long. I've got a killer to find, as well as a third victim."

Caitlyn twisted around, frowning. "Your doctor told you to take it easy."

"I will when I get this guy." When the police chief had shown up this morning in his hospital room to fill him in on what happened the past eighteen hours, he'd informed him that Greg Quinn hadn't turned up at his house. Franklin was heading over there with a search warrant. There was a good possibility Missy's body was inside. "In fact, Sean, we need to swing by the Quinns' house. Chief Franklin is there to search the place."

Sean slanted a look at Caitlyn.

"If you don't, I'll drop y'all off at Nana's, and I'll drive myself."

Caitlyn nodded, and his brother made a sharp right-hand turn, driving away from Nana's.

The previous night, neither grandmother had said much, which was most unusual, especially for Sally. "How's Nana and Sally taking this?"

"I'm afraid they're trying to figure out how to lay a trap for the killer. Every time I come into a room, they go quiet. The police officer at the house is there more to keep them inside."

"And poor Alice is being dragged into their scheme," Sean muttered as he parked in front of the Quinns' house behind a sheriff's car.

Before anyone else could move, Caitlyn jumped out and opened Ian's door, then stood in his way. "You're not going inside without me."

Ian ground his teeth. "I can walk by myself despite being wheeled out of the medical center."

She crossed her arms. "That's my condition."

Ian scooted to the edge of the seat. "I'm not in charge. You'll need to ask Chief Franklin. What he says goes."

Caitlyn nodded and offered her hand to Ian. He took it and slowly stood next to the car. His dizziness last night had abated at least, but the throbbing still hadn't. "Let's go. We'll be back in a while, Sean." He blocked out the extra jolt his walking produced by concentrating on the beautiful woman next to him with her arm around him, as though she could prevent him from collapsing. "Remember you have to convince the police chief."

"No problem. Y'all need me. I'm the only connection to all three women that we know of. Missy didn't go to our church. She spoke little of getting involved in anything in Longhorn. I got the impression she stayed home most of the time, except for coming to see me once a week."

Ian took his time mounting the porch steps. He'd realized in the short walk to the house that once he'd gone through the place, he would need to go home and rest, but only for a few hours, he hoped.

When they moved into the small foyer, the sheriff came from the living room to the left and approached Ian. "Why am I not surprised you'd show up the second they let you out of the hospital?" He shifted his amused look to Caitlyn. "And you brought your sidekick."

She chuckled. "He doesn't want anyone to know he's in pain and should be resting."

"That figures. But I can save you the grand tour. Missy Quinn isn't here, and neither is her husband. Their bedroom is the only room you might want to see. Don is in there with another officer processing it."

"Missy's body?" Ian started toward the hallway where the police chief was gathering evidence.

"Not here, but it could be the crime scene." Tom followed them.

At the doorway into the bedroom in question, Ian paused and turned toward Caitlyn. "Stay here until Chief Franklin is finished with the room."

"Actually, I could use her opinion on a note I found in the kitchen. It may be what caused her husband to kill her."

"You're sure Greg Quinn is the killer?" Caitlyn asked the sheriff.

"It's looking that way. We've got a BOLO out on him and his car. We discovered he never showed for work yesterday or the day before that." Tom, walked with Caitlyn.

Ian slowly moved into the bedroom, his attention riveted on the tousled bed with bloody sheets. As he took in the scene, he stopped at the mirror over the dresser. Written across it was one word: *Done.* Strange. This was likely scribbled across the glass before the photo was left on Sally's pillow. In that picture the usual words *Stop me!* were jotted down like the other two left for Caitlyn. So why *Done* now? Was the killer through?

Chief Franklin came out of the bathroom off the bedroom holding an evidence bag. "I'll use the brush to match DNA with the blood on the sheets."

"Was their evidence of a break-in?"

"No, not like at Kelli's house. Tom found an incomplete note in the kitchen. I think the husband discovered her trying to leave him. Maybe he killed her and then left. It looks like a lot of his clothes and two pieces of luggage are gone. I'm expanding the search for him to include the whole country. He has a good head start on us."

"He could be in Mexico by now or halfway around the world."

"Yeah, we're taking that into account."

Ian kneaded the side of his temple. "We need to find Missy's body. Any indication where it could be?"

"Other than it's not in the house, no. He could have taken her with him and dumped her in another state. I can't imagine him keeping her long."

"The smell would become overpowering. What do we know about Greg Quinn?"

"Not a lot. Surprisingly, there isn't a lot of information here. Some current bills and a few photos."

"Who did he work for?" Ian withdrew the pills he'd been given for pain and popped one into his mouth.

"The Davis Construction Company. He'd been hired six months ago right before they moved to Longhorn. Now, do me a favor—go home and rest. I'll come by later and give you a rundown of what we've found. You're pale and I can tell you're in pain."

"But—"

"No argument. We can thank God we at least know who the killer is and that he's probably long gone from here."

"Maybe." Ian rotated slowly and headed for the hallway. He'd feel better when they found Missy's body and Greg. With people he cared for touched by this, that would be the only way he would consider the case closed.

"Tell Caitlyn I'd like her to be there too. She knows Missy better than anyone else I've talked to. Every one of the Quinns' neighbors said the same thing. They rarely saw them, except Missy working in the yard from time to time. They kept to themselves."

In the hallway, Ian stopped. "How about Greg at work?"

"I'm going to visit the construction site he was working on and interview the other workers. All the boss said was he did a good job and was quiet."

As Ian made his way to the kitchen, he slowed his pace. As much as he wished otherwise, he was light-headed and needed to rest at home, then tackle the case again later today. When he found Caitlyn with the sheriff, she handed the note to Tom.

"It sounds like Missy. I knew she was troubled, but she didn't share much with me since she began coming to see me."

"How long ago was that?" Tom asked.

"Around five months ago."

"Thanks for your input, Caitlyn. You'd better go before Ian collapses."

Ian allowed Caitlyn to wrap her arm around his middle. He leaned on her a bit. "Let's go home." When he said those words to her, it felt so right. For years it had been hard for him to share himself, but with Caitlyn he realized he'd been purposefully keeping people at arm's length. He'd allowed his job to make him cynical and leery of trusting anyone. It had become easier to turn inward, leaning away from his family and people who had known him as a different person—carefree, trusting.

After reviewing all her files, Caitlyn decided to review certain patients' folders again. But not anymore today. She'd hardly left the game table in the den since she and Ian had returned from Missy Quinn's house. Earlier he'd been working on the killings, running down leads over the phone and making a list of clues involving each victim. If she hadn't insisted he take a short nap, he would still be across from her, trying to act as though his head wasn't hurting. But she saw the pain in his eyes every time she looked at him, which she was doing more than she perhaps should.

Ian Pierce was definitely a distraction, one she would relish if they weren't dealing with three murders. Something about the whole scenario nagged at her. She closed the file she'd been reading concerning a patient who had committed suicide six months ago. She'd tried to help Marcus Browning. When he'd called her and pleaded with her to stop him, she'd stayed on the phone with him while she sped to his apartment. She'd been too late. Her failure to help him ate at her. As with Byron, she tried to figure out what she could have done to have a different outcome. In seven years practicing, she'd never had a patient kill himself. The childhood abuse he'd endured had finally driven him to end his life.

She took a piece of paper and began writing down questions that plagued her. How did the killer have keys to get into her office and Granny's house? Why Jane, Kelli and Missy? Was there anything other than them being her patients that connected them? If Greg killed his wife, then why Jane and Kelli? With his departure, that pointed to him being the murderer. Before that, the killer had been cagey—one step ahead of the police, able to slip in and out of a place unnoticed.

It was a big puzzle with too many pieces missing. How in the world did Ian handle this in his job?

Her eyes stung from reading so much that day. Her mind throbbed with the pressure to come up with all the answers to end this nightmare. She folded her arms on the table and laid her head down on them. When she felt herself drifting off to sleep, she jerked upright, blinking. Her gaze lit upon her empty coffee cup, and she decided to refill it.

Shoving to her feet, Caitlyn snatched up the mug and headed for the kitchen, hearing her grandmother, Emma and Alice talking in the living room. Earlier, Sean had left to go to the ranch with Emma and check in with the foreman, which meant Ian's brother was back. She wanted to speak with him again but, with the investigation and Ian's injury, she hadn't had a chance. She'd glimpsed his panic at the hospital. He'd gone because Ian had, but he paced the whole time.

As she poured her coffee at the kitchen counter, Sean came in from the patio. "How was everything at the ranch?"

"Fine. One of our mares had a colt this morning. Nana wanted to see it. But really I think she was getting cabin fever."

"Is she the only one?"

Sean walked to the coffeepot and refilled his travel mug. "No, I was too, and I've been out today. I hope this case is over with soon."

Caitlyn leaned against the counter, cradling her cup between her hands. "You don't have to stay, so why are you?"

"Because Nana might be in danger. I may not be a Texas Ranger, but I love my grandmother and I'm capable of protecting her, especially with Ian being wounded. He acts like his head injury is no big deal, but it could be. He isn't one to ask for help."

"Is he the only Pierce who doesn't ask for help?"

One corner of his mouth hiked up. "Are you implying I don't?"

"You tell me. When you were holding the gun to your head yesterday, did you think about telling someone what was bothering you?"

Sean dropped his gaze. "No. I was thinking about Jane and me never having a chance. I was tired of losing the people I love. I was…" He turned away.

She couldn't read him. "You were what?"

"I was wondering what I had done to contribute to Jane's death."

She could identify with Sean, having questioned her patient's suicide, and yet she couldn't let Sean think he was the cause of her death. "Why would you think that? You have nothing to do with the killer. From what the police are leaning toward, it's Missy's husband."

"Why did he attack Jane?"

She planted herself in front of Sean. "I don't know. I think something was very wrong with their marriage. Her note said she was leaving him for good."

"I know what that feels like."

"You may, but you didn't kill anyone because of it."

"Technically maybe." A nerve in his cheek twitched as he placed his mug on the counter.

"What do you mean? Does it have something to do with your mother's or father's deaths?"

"I caused the riding accident that killed my mother."

"Ian told me her gelding's hoof went into a hole. As he went down, your mom was thrown and the horse fell on her. It crushed her chest, a rib puncturing her lung."

"Mom wouldn't have been out on her gelding looking for me at dusk if I hadn't run away. I fell asleep at my special fort. When I woke up, it was nearly dark, and I was hurrying back to the house when I saw the accident. If I'd just gotten up sooner or—"

Caitlyn held up her hand. "Stop right there. It was an accident. It sounds like she knew exactly where you went and was coming to get you. Things happen that are out of our control."

"I made a choice to run away because I was angry that Mom wouldn't let me spend the night at my best friend's house."

"And she made a choice to go look for you. We don't control what others do in life. Yes, we make choices, but that isn't exactly controlling our circumstances. We have to turn that over to the Lord."

"But if I'd done something different, she might be alive today."

"Or might not. Do you think your mom would want you to spend your life blaming yourself for her death?"

Sean shook his head slowly.

"It's okay to forgive yourself. That's what your mom would want."

His gaze bored into her. "It's not that simple."

She knew it wasn't, because she struggled with the same type of thing, but she had to counsel otherwise. "Why not? You've wasted many years berating yourself. It's time to live for today. Not in the past and not in the future. One we can't change and the other we don't know." If she could say this to Sean, why couldn't she follow her own words? She hadn't forgiven Byron.

Sean looked beyond her.

She swung around to find Ian standing at the kitchen door. His dark hair was mussed and the earlier pain in his eyes was gone. "How are you feeling?"

"A little better." Ian shifted his attention to Sean. "Nana said you two went to the ranch. Was there a problem?"

"Nope. Just checking in with Bud." Sean glanced at Caitlyn. "She's been helping me. Maybe she can do the same for you."

Ian frowned. "There's nothing wrong with me."

"Then, bro, why did you stay away from Longhorn for all these years? Why do you constantly move from place to place?"

"It's called a job. I go where I'm needed."

Sean crossed the room, saying, "If you say so," then disappeared into the dining room.

Ian covered the distance between them. "I heard what he said to you. How's Sean doing?"

"I think he needs to be around people right now. He's holed himself up in his house brooding and belittling himself long enough."

"Sean's always been that way when he's troubled. He clams up. I don't remember him running away the day Mom died."

"Maybe she didn't tell anyone."

"He also found Dad in his office when he collapsed. They were especially close, while I was the prodigal son."

"That's because your job took you all over Texas." But like Sean, she thought there was more to why he didn't come home often and hadn't really put down roots.

Ian reached around Caitlyn, his arm brushing against her shoulder as he took a mug down from a shelf. "Sean's right. I should have come home more often." He poured himself a coffee and started for the hallway.

Caitlyn joined him. "Why didn't you?"

He eyed her as he entered the den. "Because I didn't want to run into you—at least that was my reason at first."

"Why were you avoiding me?"

He put his mug on the game table and faced her. "The truth?"

"Always."

"Most of the time during the holidays, I subbed in for highway patrol officers who had families."

"But you missed being with your own family a lot of that time."

He closed the space between them. "Why did you break our date that night and then leave town? At the very least, I wanted to talk to you face-to-face. You didn't. What did I do wrong? I thought we had a connection that was becoming more than friendly."

How could she tell him about the biggest mistake she'd made? Only Granny knew the truth in Longhorn. "We did—we do."

Ian clasped both her hands and held them up between them—a barrier between them but also a physical link. "Then what happened?"

The pain and fear she'd suffered all those years ago surged through her, robbing her of her voice. At the time, all she'd wanted to do was hide, feeling scared and disillusioned. She'd thought she'd dealt with this in order to help others who had been raped, especially by someone they knew.

"You want to know why I didn't come home much through the years? It was the feelings of betrayal, humiliation and anger. At twenty-two, recently graduated from college and getting a job as a highway patrol officer, I wasn't as jaded and aware of the bad things people, even very close ones, could do to another. I'd just gone into law enforcement to help others who couldn't help themselves. I wanted to make a difference in a person's life."

"You have. I'm not sure how I would have coped with what has been going on without you here."

His gaze bonded with hers. "I won't let anything happen to you or our loved ones." He inhaled a deep breath and held it for a long moment, then exhaled it slowly.

"While you were away at the University of Texas, I finished getting my degree. My last semester in college I met a woman I thought I loved and wanted to marry. I even planned an elaborate dinner and gave her an engagement ring. We didn't live together, but she had a key to my apartment in Dallas. She loved to cook and often came over while I was working and fixed dinner for us. When I was working an extra-long shift, she'd go to my place and walk my dog."

As he talked about this woman he'd loved and wanted to marry, jealousy stabbed her heart. It could have been her, if not for the circumstances of her goodbye date with Byron. She had questions she would like to ask, but there was a part of her that didn't want to hear the answers. She'd made a bad decision at eighteen that had changed her whole life. She'd used her pain to help others, but still she couldn't forgive Byron.

"One night when I came home after a tense day at work, all I wanted to do was go to sleep. I couldn't. I'd been robbed. The family coin collection, handed down several generations, was stolen. It was valuable and something I wanted to continue building on for my children. I felt like I lost part of my past, and then later I discovered my bank account was wiped out too. My first thought was that I was glad Kylie hadn't come over to prepare a dinner as she'd offered. But it didn't take long to figure out who she was. That's when I did a deep background check on her and realized I wasn't her first victim. I'm a law enforcement officer, and I was fooled. You're the first person I've ever told. All I wanted to do was get far away from here. I transferred to Brownsville and buried myself in my work. I was determined no one would ever get the best of me again."

Caitlyn nodded. "I've made mistakes in reading other people's intentions. Some people are very good at hiding what they're really feeling or thinking. It can be hard for me when I'm counseling a patient. I've even had a few that I never could uncover what was really going on. Missy was like that. She wanted help but couldn't voice the real reason she came to see me. There are people who are paralyzed by their abuse and can't get beyond it, no matter how much someone wants to help."

He tugged her closer, their clasped hands still between them. "You haven't told me why you canceled our date and left town. At least as a friend, I deserved a more detailed explanation than a brief voice mail. I wanted a chance to convince you otherwise."

"I know, and that's why I left without saying anything else." The words she should have told him years ago lodged in her throat, burning, demanding release finally.

He let go of his hold on her and stepped back. "You may be good at drawing things from others, but you aren't good at letting a person get close. Why? That wasn't the way you were when we were growing up."

She stared at a spot halfway between them on the floor. *I was date-raped. Byron stripped away all my faith in people, destroyed my judgment and left me vulnerable and wounded.* She couldn't say those words. She wanted to let him get close, but...

"I have some calls to make. I won't bother you anymore. I'll make them in another room." Ian pivoted and strode off.

"Wait!" She'd held this inside for way too long. She told many patients the only way to deal with a problem was to confront it head-on, or it would grow and fester inside. Time didn't wipe it away.

He stopped at the doorway but didn't turn.

She closed the steps between them and in a low voice said, "I was raped."

Ian spun around.

She kept her gaze on his chest, afraid of what she would see in his eyes. "Remember when we started seeing each other, I told you I had a date to a dance with another guy? I went with Byron, since it had been planned for a while. We had dated off and on for several months. That night I told him I couldn't see him anymore. I knew that soon I wanted to be exclusive with you. He didn't like that. He accused me of playing games with him. He forced himself on me, no matter how many times I told him no. I…" She swallowed several times to smooth her dry throat.

Ian cradled her head between his hands and lifted her face until she looked into his eyes, a sheen in them. "I'm so sorry, Caitlyn. Did you go to the police?"

She shook her head, her tears blurring her vision. "By the time I got the courage to do that, he'd left the area. I heard he'd enlisted in the army. A couple of years later, a rumor went around Longhorn that he'd died in the Middle East. But since his family no longer lived here either, I couldn't get that confirmed. If I saw him today, I would report it, but the statute of limitations on the crime has lapsed. But…"

"He still haunts you?"

She nodded. "I didn't have any resolution with him. I didn't realize how important that was to be able to move on."

"I learned that too. I have unfinished business with

Kylie. How do you let it go and live your life without hanging on to their betrayal?"

"Granny listened to my story. She told me I needed to go to the police and then to church to pray for the ability to forgive Byron. At the time, I did neither. I still haven't forgiven him. I feel as though it hangs over me. As Christians, we're supposed to forgive. Jesus forgave us. I tell my patients to do that. But I haven't."

"I'm still searching for Kylie but, like you, even if I found her, it's too late to charge her. It was just money, and her actions still have control over me."

"I wish I had canceled my date with Byron. No telling where you and I would be now."

He slowly dipped his head toward her. When his mouth was an inch from hers, he whispered, "We have a second chance to make things right. A lot of people don't get that."

She closed her eyes and brushed her lips against his. Suddenly arms enclosed her in an embrace. His kiss, as it deepened, sought to stake a claim on her heart. She melted against him.

The sound of a chuckle behind Ian broke them apart as he swung around to face Granny and Emma, who sobered quickly. "Ian, the sheriff is here to see you and Caitlyn. Should we tell him to come back later? We don't want to interrupt y'all."

He looked sideways at Caitlyn. "We're never going to hear the end of this."

"Nope," Granny said as she moved into the room. "Emma, I think they can take a few minutes out of their—" she cleared her throat "—busy schedule to see Tom. Bring him in here while they pull themselves together."

"Granny!"

As Emma left, Caitlyn's grandmother chuckled again. "Believe me, I'd rather you two keep kissing, but I want my life back as soon as y'all figure out who is killing your patients."

"Really, Granny! If my face isn't on fire, it should be."

"All I have to say is it's about time you two saw what Emma and I have known for years."

Caitlyn exchanged a look with Ian, whose cheeks were as red as hers felt. He quickly made his way back to the table, as though they had been busy working there. Caitlyn joined him as the sheriff came into the den and closed the door, leaving Granny and Emma in the hall.

Tom hooked his thumbs in his belt. "Kelli's ex-husband, Clark, is in town. Allison called me, crying and upset."

All thoughts of her earlier embarrassment fled as Caitlyn listened to the sheriff. Could Clark Williams be the killer instead of Missy's husband, Greg?

TEN

Ian glanced at Caitlyn, all blushing washed from her cheeks, then back at Tom. "Where is Kelli's ex-husband?"

"Allison saw her father at Shop and Go right outside of town earlier, but he didn't see her. I had a deputy pick him up as he was driving toward Houston. He's bringing him in. I thought you should be in on the interview if you're up for it, Ian."

"Yes. I wonder if he was driving through or if he's been here for a while."

"That's the first question we'll ask him." The sheriff switched his attention to Caitlyn. "I'd like you there observing the interview, but not in the same room as Williams. I'll have it set up that you can have Ian ask any questions you think might help. You knew best about the volatile relationship Kelli and her husband had. Besides, Ian shouldn't be driving."

She nodded. "Where's Allison?"

"At home. I sent a deputy to her house to make sure she's all right."

"Good. Allison was caught in the middle of their divorce. She has a restraining order against him, but you and I know that often doesn't stop a person. Kelli had one too."

"Without evidence, we won't be able to hold him long for questioning." Tom strolled to the door and opened it. He laughed. "Somehow I figured you two ladies were out here. How much did you hear?"

"Tom Mason." Sally tsked. "I used to babysit you. I know secrets you wouldn't want spread around town."

He glanced over his shoulder. "Caitlyn, you must have your hands full. Good thing you're an even-tempered therapist. See you two at the station." Tom touched the brim of his cowboy hat, gave them a nod and passed by the two grandmothers in the hallway.

Emma hiked her chin up. "We were not eavesdropping. We were waiting for the door to open. We needed to know if we should hold dinner for y'all."

Ian chuckled. "How did you know we were leaving?"

Emma narrowed her eyes. "I can't help it if your voices carry."

"We may be late. We can reheat any leftovers." He gestured for Caitlyn to go ahead of him.

Sean leaned against the wall in the foyer. "I'll watch over them."

"Thanks. Maybe this will be over soon." Ian prayed it was but, as Tom had said, even if they suspected Clark was the killer, they couldn't hold him indefinitely without evidence.

Caitlyn drove Ian's SUV toward the sheriff's office as the sun was setting. Ian leaned back against the headrest. A dull headache persisted but it wasn't nearly as painful as yesterday. He wished he was at the top of his game. He should have been more present with Caitlyn instead of napping, but he hadn't got a good night's rest in the regional medical center, especially with someone coming in to check on him every hour.

He closed his eyes as passing headlights lit up the interior of his vehicle. The brightness still hurt his eyes. A picture of Caitlyn trying to fight off Byron filled his mind, and he balled his hands. Having dealt with rape victims in his job, he'd seen firsthand the trauma women went through. And to think Caitlyn had basically handled it by herself fueled his anger at Byron even more. Too bad Byron had never faced any consequences for what he had done.

He couldn't believe he'd shared his story about Kylie. He'd never told anyone, but then he shouldn't be surprised that, if he was going to confide in anyone, he'd pick Caitlyn. She made it easy to talk. Her job was perfect for her.

When Caitlyn made a turn and slowed down, Ian opened his eyes to find they were in the parking lot next to the sheriff's station.

She withdrew the key from the ignition. "I'd like to go see Allison after you interview her father. She may need someone to talk to. Kelli told me how hard Allison took the truth about her dad and the divorce."

"Allison didn't know about Kelli being abused?"

"Kelli tried to shield her and thought she had, but I wouldn't be surprised that Allison knew something was seriously wrong."

"I've talked with Allison about her dad, but seeing her after I interview him, I might have additional questions for her." Ian opened his door, climbed from the SUV and met Caitlyn on the sidewalk to the station. He took her hand. "Ready?"

"Yes."

Tom greeted them. "I thought the deputy would have Williams here by now, but there was an accident on the highway. He should be here anytime now. Y'all can stay in my office, and I'll come get you when he's brought in."

As the sheriff escorted them toward his office, the back door to the station opened and a deputy brought in a handcuffed Williams. The man's angry stare zoomed in on Caitlyn.

The suspect cursed and plunged forward. "She ruined my marriage, and now she's accusing me of killing my wife!"

The deputy restrained Williams and pinned him against the wall with the help of another officer. The suspect wore a T-shirt that suggested he must work out a lot. He reminded Ian of a linebacker on his high school team, nicknamed The Mower.

"Well, she's a liar! I'll get the truth out of her," Williams shouted, wrenching his body from side to side, breaking free and launching himself at her.

Ian stepped closer, putting his body in front of Caitlyn.

As the two officers subdued him again, the sheriff said, "Get him in the interview room and secure him. Stay with him."

Once Williams had disappeared down the hallway, Ian moved to the side and grasped her arms. "Okay?"

"I knew he blamed me for the divorce but, after six months, I'd have hoped he'd calmed down some."

"Has Williams been formally charged?" Ian asked Tom.

"Yes. He wouldn't pull over when the deputy flashed his lights. Instead, he sped away, going thirty to forty miles over the speed limit while intoxicated. We can hold him for sure until court Monday on that."

"Good." Caitlyn's comment came out on a long breath. "Kelli described some of his attacks when he was drinking. He was a mean drunk. I can't believe she stayed with him as long as she did."

"I can't believe he didn't kill her sooner." Ian slipped his arm around Caitlyn. She still trembled from the encounter with Williams.

"Let's get this over with. I'll feel better when he's locked in a cell and hopefully calmed down." Tom opened the first door in the corridor. "This is where you will be, Caitlyn. I'm posting a deputy outside the room as a precaution."

"I appreciate that."

"I'll send Deputy Altom in to hook you up so you can speak to Ian if there's something he needs to ask."

As the door closed on the room where Caitlyn was with the officer, Ian stuck his earpiece in and tested it to make sure it worked. Then he and the sheriff entered the interview room, two other deputies standing with a seated Williams between them. The suspect was handcuffed to the sturdy table. His glare bored into the sheriff and Ian as they sat down across from him. One deputy left, while the other positioned himself behind Williams. The reek of alcohol wafted toward Ian.

"How many drinks have you had?" the sheriff asked.

"One. I was heading home. A guy can drink one. I'm not drunk."

"But you refused to do the Breathalyzer."

"That's my right. I was doing nuthin' wrong when your deputy tried to stop me. I'm gonna file a harass-

ment suit against you." Williams scanned the small interview room, pressing his lips tightly together.

"We stopped you because you are a person of interest in a murder case."

Williams's eyes bugged out. "You think I killed my
wife!"

"Ex-wife." When Ian interjected that, the wrath of
Williams turned on him.

This time his glare cut through Ian. "Who are you?"

"I'm Texas Ranger Pierce, heading up an investigation of the three murders that have occurred recently
in Longhorn. Your ex-wife was the first victim. We've
been looking for you. I understand you don't live here
anymore. Why are you back?"

"It's a free country. I can go where I want."

"How long have you been here?"

Williams shrugged.

"The restraining order restricts how close you can
be to your ex-wife and daughter. You seem like a guy
that picks and chooses what laws you obey. Did you see
Kelli while you were here?"

"I came for her funeral tomorrow. She was my wife
for twenty-five years."

"Then why were you heading out of town?"

"It's a free country. I can drive where I want." His
hands clutched together, Williams poured out hostility.

Ian leaned back in his chair as though he had not a
care in the world. "Where are you staying in town?"

"Forgot its name." Sweat beaded Williams's forehead.

"How long have you been in town?"

"You already asked me that." Williams's words
slurred together.

"And you didn't answer me. It's a simple question."

"I just arrived today. Let's see." Williams held up one hand with one finger bent at the knuckle. "That means not even one day."

"Ask him if he's seen Sam Baker." Caitlyn's voice came through the earpiece. "They did everything together, according to Kelli."

"Have you seen Sam?"

Williams's eyebrows scrunched together, almost forming a straight line. His look highlighted his blood-shot eyes. "Who?"

"Your best friend, Sam Baker."

"Oh, you mean Sammy. Of course I've seen him. He'll vouch for me. You ain't pinning Kelli's murder on me."

"Then tell me where you were this week from Monday evening to eleven o'clock Wednesday morning." Although the ME had narrowed Kelli's death to early Tuesday morning, Ian wanted to know Williams's whereabouts for the times of both Jane's and Williams's ex-wife's murder.

Williams smirked. "Sleeping in a bed and drinking in a bar. Neither against the law."

"Sheriff, do you have any questions for him?" Ian decided Williams needed to stay in jail for a while before being questioned again.

"Nope."

"Good." Williams stood up, hunched over because of his hands being cuffed to the table. "I need a ride to Sammy's house."

Ian slowly rose. "Not going to happen. You're staying in a cell until you're brought before a judge to set your bail."

"You can't charge me! You have no evidence I was drinking." Williams jerked on the chains. "I want outta here!" Sweat rolled down his face. His chest rose and fell rapidly as he looked from side to side. "I need fresh air. Now!"

"Kelli told me Clark could freak out when he thought he was trapped."

Caitlyn's words made sense to Ian. He motioned to Tom and stepped away to whisper to the sheriff, "He'll need two or three guards to take him back to his cell. He doesn't like to feel trapped so he may try to escape."

Tom gave Ian one nod and opened the door, signaling the two deputies in the corridor to enter the room.

As before, Williams struggled to get away from his three-officer escort, stopping halfway to the hallway to glare at the two-way mirror. "I hope the killer stops *you*."

Ian stepped into his line of sight, feet apart and arms crossed over his chest. Once the suspect disappeared around the corner with Tom following, Ian hurried to the room Caitlyn was in. The door flung open before he had a chance to open it.

She went into his arms, her body shaking. "His behavior is exactly how Kelli described it when he would drink. Then he would sober up for a while and act like the perfect husband."

"Dr. Jekyll and Mr. Hyde."

"Yes, exactly. When he was in his 'Dr. Jekyll' mode, she would start to think he was going to change. But he never did. I'd like to go to Allison's now and see how she is."

"I hope she can tell us about Sammy Baker."

"All I really know is he's the husband of Kelli's boss

Nell Baker and Kelli's relationship with her employer was precarious at times."

"All the more reason to pay the Bakers a visit tomorrow." Ian walked toward the large room at the sheriff's office. "I'll call Tom later and see when he wants to interview Williams again. He never asked for a lawyer so that's promising. After being in jail overnight, he might want to talk, especially when he's sober."

"I hope he will. I'm going stir-crazy myself. I'm used to being out and about during the day. I'm not used to having a bodyguard."

"And I'm usually not a bodyguard. I'm often the one out running down leads in a case." He opened the SUV's passenger door, the light illuminating her beautiful face. "I have to admit I'm kinda liking this."

She slid onto the front seat, slanting him a smile that made his heartbeat race. For a short time, he forgot about the dull throb in his head and savored this moment with Caitlyn. He wanted more—especially when they wouldn't have to look over their shoulders all the time.

Caitlyn sat next to Allison in her living room. "Tell me about Sammy Baker and your dad."

"They have been buddies for as long as I can remember, and that's been the problem."

"Why do you say that, Allison?" Ian asked, seated in a chair across from them.

"Every time he was with Sammy, he came home drunk, yelling and hitting Mom. She tried to keep it from me, but I knew."

"Does your father know Jane Shephard or Missy

Quinn?" Ian leaned forward, his hands clasped, elbows on his thighs.

"Dad used to work at the Shephard ranch, so I guess he did. Missy Quinn? I don't know her. All I know is she's missing."

Caitlyn felt the tension radiating off Allison next to her. Something wasn't right. "Since Missy only moved here five months ago and Clark moved away over six months ago, I'd say probably not, unless he came back to Longhorn before now. Have you seen your dad here in town before today?"

Allison lowered her chin and stared at a spot on her lap.

"Allison?" Caitlyn glanced at Ian, who gave her a nod. "What's wrong?"

"I should have told you. I'm pretty sure my dad was at my mom's house on Tuesday. I saw the Chevy he was driving today parked near my mom's place on Tuesday. I even called her, thinking maybe she didn't go to see her friend. No one answered, and then when I went to look at the vehicle out front, it was gone. I didn't know that was Dad's car until today, but I should have said something."

"So he was in town at least on Tuesday?"

Allison nodded. "Did he kill her?" Her voice quavered, tears shining in her eyes.

Ian stood. "We don't know, but I won't stop looking for your mother's killer."

His determination reassured Caitlyn she wasn't alone. He was here to help her and other women in Longhorn. The thought comforted her.

Caitlyn turned to Allison. "He'll be in jail for a couple of days, and if he can't make bail, he'll be there longer. In the meantime, the case is the top priority for the police and the sheriff."

"And the Texas Rangers too." Ian surveyed the house. "Is there anyone you and your two children can stay with until the case is resolved?"

"My in-laws. They live in Paris and would love to see the grandkids. I wish my husband hadn't been deployed overseas. He never liked my father and wouldn't even allow him in our house. I'll take my girls out of school until I know they're safe." Allison pushed to her feet and hugged Caitlyn when she rose. "Thank you for what you did for Mom. The funeral is tomorrow, and I'm glad Dad won't be able to attend. I was worried he would want to. I don't need any more upset."

As they walked to the front door, Caitlyn said, "We'll be there, and if you need anything or to just talk, call me." She took a business card out of her purse and wrote her personal number on the back.

"Thank you." Allison switched her attention to Ian. "If I can think of anything that will help you with the case, I'll call you. I still have your card."

"I appreciate that."

Caitlyn made her way to Ian's SUV in silence. There was something she was missing. Clark could have killed his wife, but why Jane and Missy? And where was Greg Quinn? Dead too?

She massaged the tips of her fingers into her temple. "How do you put all the clues together to come up with the perpetrator of a crime?"

"A lot of them aren't very smart and trip themselves up. But in this case, it isn't that easy. I keep thinking I'm not looking at this from the right angle."

"Me too. When we get to Emma's, I want to go through some files again, then start over tomorrow."

"About tomorrow. I don't know if it's a good thing for you to go to the funeral. The killer has involved you throughout."

"You'll be with me. I'll be fine. I can help you with information about the people attending. And the same about Jane's funeral on Monday afternoon."

"Are you doing your show on Monday?"

"Yes. His break-in forced me to cancel my appointments for this week, but my talk show is heard around the country. I'm not letting this man control my life."

"The governor will be at the funeral on Monday. There will be several Texas Rangers there too."

"Still no sighting of Missy's husband?"

"No, not him or his car. No signals from either of the Quinns' cell phones and no hits on their credit cards."

Caitlyn parked in Emma's driveway. "What if the killer ended up murdering both of them?"

"That would be changing his MO, but the husband could have interrupted the guy, and he had to murder Greg Quinn too." Ian exited the SUV and met up with Caitlyn on the sidewalk leading to his grandmother's house.

While she unlocked the door, Ian exchanged a few words with the deputy standing on the porch.

"I'm starving. Let's get our dinner and take it into the den." Ian followed her into the house and paused at the entrance into the living room. "Have Nana and Sally gone to bed?" he asked Sean, who was watching television.

"About fifteen minutes ago. Did Clark confess to killing his wife?"

Ian shook his head. "We're going to grab something to eat and then work in the den for a while. Probably not long though. I didn't realize how late it is."

Caitlyn crossed the living room. "My stomach knew it was way past dinnertime. Do you want anything to eat, Sean?"

"No, Nana already tried to fatten me up." He patted his stomach. "And partially succeeded."

Caitlyn entered the kitchen and headed for the refrigerator, where she found two plates of spaghetti. "Can you stick them in the microwave?? I'll go get a few files I wanted to review again. We can work in here instead."

"Sure."

In the den, Caitlyn picked up four files of women she was currently helping. As she made her way back to the kitchen, she slowed her steps, weariness weaving through her body. The long day—week—was catching up with her. Glasses of iced tea and one plate of dinner were on the table, while the microwave beeped. She needed to eat something, but even that task seemed monumental.

Ian joined her and set the last of the food down. "Why those files?"

"They are most likely the killer's possible targets from all my patients. In my opinion. I wasn't even sure if I should do that kind of conjecture. What if I'm wrong?"

"I look at the pieces of evidence I have and make educated guesses from my experiences all the time. I've been wrong but also often right."

"I just don't want to see anyone else murdered." With a long sigh, Caitlyn bowed her head and blessed their food. "Using brain power makes me hungrier than when I work out."

Ian gestured toward the stack of folders. "So why these four patients?"

"Their problems have similarities to the ones Jane, Kelli and Missy had. Both Jane and Kelli lived alone, which makes coming after them easier. The one time he deviated, it's possible the husband interrupted and had to be killed, which no doubt caused problems."

"Or it has nothing to do with being single. Until we find Greg Quinn, he's the prime suspect in the case, although Clark's a good one too." He took a bite of the spaghetti.

"From what Kelli told me about Clark and what I've seen, I'm not sure he's capable of planning these murders. He's impulsive."

"I have my doubts too, but we still have to investigate him and rule him out. The killer is bold and cunning. He's getting in and out of places with no detection. I don't think this is a rash decision on his part. He possibly has been planning it for a while."

Caitlyn tapped the top file she'd brought into the kitchen. "These four patients and the victims all have similar build, coloring and personalities. They aren't inherently assertive. Of course, we don't know if the killer will only target women I work with, but it's a place to start. Of the four I chose, two are single and two are married. I want to warn them to be careful."

"Okay. We should have someone watching them, even though the case is already stretching our manpower. But we need to look at all the evidence again and see if we've missed anything."

She stared at her uneaten food. "I agree, but I don't

think I can make sense of anything right now. We can do that first thing tomorrow morning. Once I sat down to eat, I realized I wouldn't be able to do much more." She smiled. "That was my mistake. Sitting down."

Ian chuckled. "I've gone fast and furious and then sat down for just a moment and couldn't get up. Exhaustion can do that to you. And to tell you the truth, I could use the extra rest myself."

"I don't know how you get any, when people's lives are at stake." Caitlyn finally took her first bite of dinner.

"I've discovered I do my best thinking when I'm sleeping. I've gone to bed with a problem nagging me and have awakened with a new perspective. Even God took time to rest after creating the world."

"True." Caitlyn ate another forkful.

"Tomorrow we'll also need to look at people who might have a problem with you. Someone could really be after you."

"I know. Over the years, I've worked with patients who have difficult issues. I've been able to help many but, like I said, some I haven't."

He reached across the table and cupped her hand. His gaze trapped hers. "And I've had criminals get away with what they did. Most of my cases are solved, but a few aren't. One I know who did the crime, but we can't get enough evidence to take him to court. That's hard to live with. I still go back to it from time to time. One day I hope to find that evidence."

"My most difficult one is the young man who committed suicide while under my care. There was so much he wasn't telling me about a bad situation. In his note he left, he wrote about being abused as a child, and he couldn't deal with the memories anymore. He never told me that. He'd mentioned being bullied as a child by kids at school but said he was okay now. No matter what I did, I was hitting a wall with him, although I didn't think he would kill himself. Some patients take a while to feel comfortable to share why they're really coming to see me."

"Does his family live in Longhorn?" Ian squeezed her hand gently, then slid his away.

"No. He lived alone. He didn't talk about his family. They lived in San Antonio."

"I'd like to look into them. When did this happen?" He picked up his glass and sipped his iced tea.

"Six months ago. His name was Marcus Browning."

"Any other person who might have a grudge against you?"

"Well, other than Clark, I'd need to think about it." While finishing her dinner, Caitlyn ran through her current patients first and then ones she'd seen in the past few years. "There was a boyfriend of a young woman who broke it off, and he thought I was the reason. He came to the office last year in the guise of a new patient. He was quite angry at me, but in the end, he calmed down and became my patient. He still is. The young woman moved away. I can't see him as the killer."

"What's his name?"

"Paul Nichols. I can't tell you anything else about him. He would freak out if he thought the police were investigating him."

"I can look into him quietly." Ian stood and took their plates over to the sink.

Caitlyn brought the glasses to the counter, and as he rinsed the dishes, she put them in the dishwasher. As they walked from the kitchen, she said, "I'll keep thinking about people I've interacted with to see if there's anyone else."

"I'm going to look into Byron Woods. I have a connection in Washington. If he died while in the service, I'll find it out. If not, I want to know where he is."

"That happened seventeen years ago. Why would he come after me now?"

"Because you know what he did. What if he was afraid of you coming forward to accuse him, even though it's too late to prosecute him? People in the limelight have their life broadcasted all over the place."

"He isn't in the limelight."

"But he could be down the road. We have to consider it." Ian paused in the hallway. "I won't say anything unless I find him, if that'll make you feel better."

I need to forgive Byron whether he's alive or dead—somehow. He's affected my life long enough.

"Keep me informed of anything you find about him."

At the door of her bedroom, she swung around to say good-night. His proximity stole away the words, while his gaze drew her toward him. She wanted him to kiss her again. Suddenly she needed reassurances from him that he still cared about her, even knowing what happened that summer after graduation.

He started to turn away, stopped and wrapped his arms around her, bringing her up flat against him. "I'm glad we finally talked about seventeen years ago. I'm glad I'm here finally. I shouldn't have stayed away so long."

"I'm glad too." She laced her fingers together behind his neck and tugged him toward her.

His mouth came down on hers as though suppressed emotions were finally released and he was demanding a second chance for them. She met his fervent kiss with her own, pouring out all the feelings she'd kept locked away for years.

When he backed away, she didn't want to let him go, but they both needed to rest and be ready to go through the case tomorrow—before another woman was murdered.

"Good night, Caitlyn."

She went on tiptoe, gave him a quick kiss, then hurried into the bedroom she was sharing with Granny, leaning against the closed door with the widest smile on her face.

Good thing Granny was asleep or she would keep her awake, interrogating her about why she looked as if she was floating on a cloud.

A shaft of light streamed through the partially open curtains that her grandmother left that way, so she could see her path to the bed without turning on the overhead light. She felt her way to the window and peeked out before drawing them.

Facing Granny's house, Caitlyn glimpsed a dark shadow near the patio in the backyard. She closed the drapes, then fumbled her way to the door. Out in the hallway, she crossed to Ian's room and knocked.

When he answered the door, she said, "There's someone at Granny's."

ELEVEN

"How do you know?" Ian stepped back into his room and grabbed his weapon and flashlight.

"I was closing the curtains when I saw a dark shadow by the patio. It's not an animal. It's upright like a man."

Ian headed down the hallway. "You stay here."

"Don't go alone. Take the officer outside with you. Remember what happened at Granny's house."

"He needs to stay here guarding you."

She paused at the the living room. "Sean is here. He'll protect us."

Sean rose. "What's going on?"

Had the killer come back? He hoped he had, so this nightmare would be over. "There may be an intruder at Sally's house. Call the police to send backup." Ian opened the front door.

Sean came into the foyer. "I'll take care of the ladies but have the officer go with you, or I will—and you can't stop me." He moved to the exit as though he would follow Ian if he had to.

Ian was very familiar with Sean's stubborn expression, and he didn't have time to argue with him. "Officer, there may be an intruder on the property next door." Ian pointed in the direction of Granny's house. "We need to check it out."

As Ian left, Caitlyn's tensed shoulders sagged with relief as she stood next to Sean. Ian didn't want her to worry about him.

"Caitlyn said there was someone in the backyard by the patio," he said quietly. Ian rounded the side of Sally's house ahead of the officer, using the security light at his grandmother's place to guide his steps.

He opened the four-foot gate and pressed himself close to the house as he crept to the corner. When he peeked at the patio, he spied the dark shadow near the post that had to be what Caitlyn had seen. He couldn't tell if it was a person, but he had to treat it that way until he knew for sure.

Signaling the officer to follow him, Ian stepped into the backyard in plain view of the dark shadow. With feet braced a part, Ian held his gun pointed at the apparent intruder while his flashlight illuminated the area.

Revealing a plastic female doll about six feet tall.

The hairs on the nape of his neck rose. The dark shadow might not be an intruder, but someone had put it here. The killer? "When was the last time you checked Sally's backyard?"

"An hour ago. As per Chief Franklin's orders, I also shine my light over this area each time too, and a plastic doll wasn't there at that time."

Ian edged closer to the dark shadow. While inspecting the rest of the yard, he motioned for the policeman to investigate the back part. Ian swung his flashlight toward the French doors—closed. But were they locked? He approached, gripped the knobs and turned them. They were secure.

Quickly he trailed his light over each window and tested them. All locked. Finally, he returned his attention to the plastic doll, while the officer completed his search. Taped on its chest was a note with the words *Stop me!* on it. But no photo. He moved closer and looked under the note. Still no picture.

What kind of game was the killer playing? Was he watching him right now?

Fifteen minutes after Ian left to check her grandmother's patio, Caitlyn paused at the living room picture window and glanced at the three patrol cars in front of Granny's house. Where was Ian? Was he all right? What happened?

She couldn't take not knowing. "Sean, I'm going over there. You stay here with Emma, Alice and Granny." She started for the front door.

Sean moved fast and blocked her exit. "No. That would force me to go with you and leave our grandmothers alone. Do you want me to do that?"

She shook her head. "But what if—"

"Don't go there. We haven't heard any gunshots. The police arrived quickly."

"But yesterday the guy hit him over his head."

"This time he has an officer with him and is alert to the possibility of being attacked."

She started pacing while Sean leaned against the wall near the living room entrance. "How can you be so calm after this past week?"

"No one wants this guy more than me. He killed Jane and came after my brother." He held out his shaky hand. "And I'm not calm," he gave her a sheepish smile, "but don't tell Ian. I'm the big brother. I'm supposed to protect the family."

"I hope when this is over you'll come see me. I think I can help you. If not me, I can recommend someone for you to see."

"I'll think about it."

"That's—"

The sound of a key being inserted into the front door cut off Caitlyn's reply. She hurried into the foyer, but Sean shielded her with his body. She tensed.

"I'm coming inside," Ian said on the other side of the closed door.

Relief surged through her, replacing the fear she'd dealt with since Ian went over to Granny's house. When he entered, she skirted around Sean and threw her arms around Ian. "I've been worried. Did you catch the guy?"

"No, but I captured a female plastic doll."

She pulled back. "Really?"

"Yes. Once forensics is finished with it, do you want me to bring it here?"

She laughed and punched Ian playfully in the upper arm. But quickly the realization someone had placed it in the backyard sobered her. "The killer left it?"

"Yes, with a *Stop me!* note but no photo. The back of the note had a big question mark on it."

She blew out a long breath. The implication sent a shiver down her length.

"The police are checking every square foot of the yard and house, as well as Nana's yard."

"I'm glad Emma, Alice and Granny are asleep. I don't want them to know about the plastic doll."

"To be on the safe side, Sean and I need to go through

this house too." Ian glanced at his older brother, who had retreated to the living room.

The idea the murderer could be in Emma's house or even the yard caused Caitlyn's heartbeat to speed up. "Wouldn't we have heard something?"

"I'm not assuming anything with this killer. We'll leave Nana's and your bedrooms to last."

"What do I do?" Caitlyn crossed her arms, suddenly chilly.

"Stay here. This is just a precaution." Ian guided her into the living room. "Relax. The sheriff is loaning a deputy to Chief Franklin to stay outside in the backyard. He'll also keep an eye on Sally's house."

"Good."

As Sean and Ian went in different directions, Caitlyn paced again, exhausted but also wired. Would she get any sleep tonight? If she didn't, she wasn't sure she'd be able to put two coherent words together tomorrow. She counted her steps to keep her mind away from the fact she was yet again drawn into this case by the killer.

When they returned to the living room, Caitlyn stopped and swept around to face them. "Everything okay?"

Sean nodded.

"You and I will check out the bedroom where you and your grandmother are staying. Sean will go through Alice and Emma's room."

"What are we going to tell them?" Sean asked.

"The truth," Ian said to his brother.

"We could always move to our ranch."

"The house is too big. It would be harder to defend."

Caitlyn sucked in a deep breath at Ian's words, as though they were caught in the middle of a war—

because of her. "You think the killer is going to attack us here?"

"I don't know, but we have to be prepared for the possibility."

Caitlyn looked at Sean. "Don't tell Alice and Emma that. They'll worry enough with the fact the killer was in Granny's backyard."

The trio walked down the hallway, first inspecting Sean and Ian's bedroom before moving on to the other two. Caitlyn wished they could check out hers in the dark and hoped that Granny didn't wake up. But when they entered, Ian flipped on the overhead light while Caitlyn headed for the bed.

As she expected, Granny shot up in bed, blinking. "What's going on?" She leaned around Caitlyn. "Why's Ian in here? What happened?"

Caitlyn told Granny what she saw and what Ian had found on her patio. "The police have gone through your house and yard again. The killer didn't get inside."

"I don't think I'll ever feel safe in that place again."

Ian paused at the end of the bed. "Everything is fine in here. We went through Nana's just as a precaution. I hope you can go back to sleep."

"Sure, young man. I'm used to being scared half to death, then calmly lying down and going back to the dream I was having. What did you think? That the killer was going to climb through the window without me knowing? I'm a light sleeper."

Caitlyn put her hand on Granny's shoulder. "Try to go back to sleep. I'll be back in a few minutes to go to bed myself." And she didn't want to deal with her grandmother's questions she no doubt would have about tonight. Caitlyn waited until Granny had lain down and pulled the covers up to her shoulders before she rose and followed Ian into the corridor.

Down the hall, Sean closed the door on his grandmother's bedroom. "Everything's okay. That's my cue to go to bed."

Noting the lines on Ian's tired face, Caitlyn said, "You should go too."

"Not until you do."

"I am. Granny won't go to asleep until I do. I wanted to ask you one question. Do you think the killer has murdered a fourth victim? Those notes usually show up when he has. The question mark might mean we have to guess who it is."

"As I said, no photo. I don't know exactly why he left that note with the question mark, but he may genuinely be wanting you to stop him."

"I don't know who the killer is. How can I stop him?"

He grasped her upper arms and brought her closer. "All I know is that I don't want you alone. His fixation on you is growing."

She shuddered. Ian rubbed his hands up and down her arms.

"Where I go you go, and where you go I go. I'm not losing you after all these years." He brushed his mouth across hers, whispering, "Good night."

He stepped back. She wanted to throw her arms around him and never let go, but the next few days would be difficult and, without rest, impossible.

She moved to the door and slipped into Granny's bedroom.

"It's about time you came in here. Now I can go back to sleep," Granny murmured from the bed.

Caitlyn quickly got ready for bed, then slid under the

sheet and coverlet. Within five minutes, Granny's soft snores indicated she was okay. But Caitlyn wasn't. She was sure she knew the killer. So why couldn't she find him? Put an end to the terror in Longhorn?

During the midpoint commercial of her Monday radio show, Caitlyn leaned back in her chair, closing her eyes for a few seconds. Each listener's call brought fear that it was the killer. Saturday night he had left a plastic doll at her grandmother's house that looked surprisingly like her. She was walking around with a bull's-eye on her back. Why her?

As she reached for her glass of water, her hand shook. She took a long sip, her gaze embracing Ian's in the producer's booth. He smiled, its warmth chasing away the chill buried deep in her as though it were part of her marrow. She wasn't alone.

When the commercial ended, Caitlyn sat forward and said into the microphone, "Welcome back. Let's see who our next caller is." Her finger hovered over the on button a moment longer than usual. When she finally pressed it, she continued. "This is Dr. Caitlyn Rhodes. You're on the air. How can I help you?"

For a few seconds, silence ruled. Caitlyn stiffened. Was it the killer? Her pulse pounded through her body.

"I don't know what to do. I don't think I can go through with my wedding this month."

Not the killer. Relief filled her. "Why do you feel that way?" Caitlyn rolled her tensed shoulders and dived into helping her caller.

After the young woman had hung up, Caitlyn took another caller and relaxed even more, throwing herself into what she loved doing the most: helping others. Ten minutes to the end of her program, she answered her the next one.

Halfway through her spiel, the familiar disguised voice interrupted her. "You don't know how to stop me. What kind of therapist are you? Three people are dead because of you."

The killer talked rapidly, not allowing her to say anything, then hung up, leaving Caitlyn stunned, still trying to assimilate the question. Melanie signaled for her to continue while the door opened and Ian entered the studio.

He sat in a chair next to her and rubbed his hand up and down her upper arm.

She blinked and took the next listener on the line, somehow managing to say the right words. In between that caller and the next one, Ian received a text and he showed her: Using Missy Quinn's phone but not enough time to trace.

When Caitlyn finished her program, she slumped back into the chair. A loud *swoosh* of air blew from her mouth. But no words came to her mind to say.

Ian lifted her chin and turned her in her chair so that she was looking into his face. "I've heard you with your listeners, and I can say you're a caring therapist who wants the best for the people you work with. Your words matter."

"The call from the killer means it isn't Clark Williams. He's in jail and wouldn't have Missy's cell phone on him. For Allison's sake, I'm glad it wasn't him. So, either Greg Quinn or someone we haven't thought of is the real murderer. And we don't know where he is."

"Yep. Is there a reason Greg would be after you too?

His message has changed. He's blaming you for everything."

"I can't imagine why he would be after me. Missy barely talked about him."

"Let's go to Nana's and get ready for the funeral."

"That sounds great. I didn't sleep very well last night. I'm going to take a nap before we go." Caitlyn rose at the same time Ian did.

He moved in front of her and cradled her face between his large hands. "I'm not going to let this maniac get to you. He's not going to win."

"Right now, I feel he is. Three women are dead, and he's affecting my practice." The blood on the sheets in Missy's bedroom was her type, and the police were waiting on a DNA test to confirm it all belonged to Missy. Surviving that much blood loss would have been unlikely. "I hope at least for Missy's family that her body is found. Have y'all been able to find her next of kin besides her husband?"

"Not yet. There wasn't a lot of information at her house. We're still working on connections through Greg's family."

"Missy said that they were both from Texas but had moved around as kids and as a couple."

"That's what we've run into. Let's go." Ian opened the door and waited until Caitlyn walked into the hallway, where Melanie was waiting for her.

Her producer hugged her. "What do you want to do about the show the rest of the week?"

"I'll be here on Wednesday. I can't let this killer win. But I am going to have you vet the callers. My listeners can't be pulled into his game. He doesn't want help."

There had been a time she'd hoped to get the man to turn himself in before killing someone else.

"I can do that. I'll see you at the funeral later today. I think the whole town is turning out for it."

When Caitlyn settled in Ian's SUV, she asked, "Is Sean going to Jane's funeral?"

"The last time I talked to him, he wasn't sure. I thought it was because of Jack and Sean's relationship at first, but now I don't know."

"I'll talk to him. He needs to go and say goodbye to Jane."

"He wouldn't go to Mom's, and I had a hard time getting him to Dad's. He insisted on a closed casket at our father's funeral."

"He needs the closure."

"Yeah, but he'll never admit it."

Ten minutes later, Ian pulled into his grandmother's driveway. "I want to go a little early."

Every time she was outside she panned her surroundings, as she'd seen Ian do. This time was different. A sense of being watched crept through her. She hurried her steps, nodding at Officer Collins as she ducked inside. Both Granny and Emma were standing in the living room doorway. By their serious expressions, she knew that they had listened to the show.

Granny moved to her and took a hand. "Honey, don't believe a word that man said today. None of this is your fault. It's his." She tugged her toward the couch while Emma put her arm around Caitlyn.

She stopped Granny from continuing in the same vein. "I'm taking a nap. Wake me up in an hour?"

Her grandmother's mouth formed a tight straight

line but she released Caitlyn's hand. "Don't let him get to you."

"I'm not. I just need rest." She backed away from the two women and bumped into Ian. Gasping, she whirled around. "I didn't hear you come into the house."

"I'll walk you to your room."

She glanced at Emma. "Where's Sean?"

"Out back. I think he's going stir-crazy like we are," Emma said.

"I'll talk with him," Ian murmured into Caitlyn's ear. "If he hasn't changed his mind, then you can talk to him. Get some sleep. I'm not going to let anything happen to you."

Granny and Emma exchanged a quizzical look.

Emma set her fists on her hips. "It's not polite to whisper. What are y'all hiding?"

Ian looked up at the ceiling, shaking his head. "Sorry, Nana. Nothing." Then he guided Caitlyn toward the bedrooms.

At her door, she peered up into his handsome face. "Thanks for rescuing me."

"Anytime." He smiled, kissed her forehead and started down the corridor.

Caitlyn removed her shoes and collapsed on the bed, hoping sleep would whisk her away from her reality. As she finally felt herself sinking deeper into a dream state, the doorbell rang, jerking her totally awake. She rolled over and glanced at the digital clock. She still had half an hour until she needed to get ready for the funeral. Her eyelids drifted closed.

"Get off my property, or I'll have these officers arrest you for trespassing!"

Caitlyn groaned and sat up. Was that Emma yelling?

She left her bedroom, padded down the hall and peeked around the corner into the foyer. The front door was wide-open with Ian and Sean standing in the entrance. Emma and Granny were behind them.

"What's going on?" Caitlyn ambled forward, smoothing the wrinkles in her blouse, then running her fingers through her hair, as she realized she looked disheveled.

Granny turned in Caitlyn's direction, her forehead creased with deep lines of anger. "Reporters trying to camp out in Emma's yard."

"Why?" Caitlyn asked although she was pretty sure what the reason was.

"They want to interview you. There are at least twenty of them. Some are from out of state."

Finally, the brothers stepped back, and Ian shut the front door. "Chief Franklin is here and forcing them to leave the yard. Instead they're standing around on the sidewalk, ready to mob anyone who comes out of this house."

"How do we get to the funeral? I'm not talking to the press." She didn't want to do anything to encourage the killer. Caitlyn entered the living room and made her way to the front window to peek outside while staying behind the curtains.

"The chief's giving them an update in the case. Hopefully that will satisfy them. They've been hanging out at the Shephards' ranch for the past day. When they heard your show today, most of them came here."

"Do you think they'll go to the funeral?"

"Probably."

"Then I'll have to deal with them."

Ian frowned. "Yeah, but the police will be there too

and will try to minimize their presence. The police are working with the Shephards."

"Sean, are you going to the funeral?"

He nodded at Caitlyn.

"Good. I'm going to get ready. If there's a way to leave this house without the press knowing, I'd appreciate it, especially if we can make it look like I'm staying here and not going to the funeral. At least the number of reporters will be less there if some are camped outside the house."

Ian took both of her hands. "I think I've got a plan. Go get ready while I work out the logistics."

The confident look in his eyes bolstered her. "Thanks." She headed for her bedroom. God was with her.

I can do this, and if dealing with the press is part of it, that's all right.

She quickly donned black pants, a white blouse and a matching dark jacket, as she'd done with Kelli's funeral yesterday. Then she slipped on black flats and ran a brush through her shoulder-length hair. She was afraid that, when they found Missy's body, she would have to wear these clothes again.

When she returned to the living room, Granny, Emma and Alice were ready to go and stood near Sean. "Where's Ian?"

"I'm here." He strode through the dining room and stopped next to Caitlyn. "I've set everything up. Are y'all ready to leave?" he asked the four women and Sean. "Ignore the reporters and get into the car as quickly as possible."

With Sean leading the older women, they filed out

of the house, then Ian closed and locked the front door before Caitlyn could leave.

"Aren't we going?"

"Not that way." He hurried toward the kitchen door, let Caitlyn go first outside, then joined her on the patio, nodding toward the deputy covering the area.

Caitlyn spied a stepladder at the back of the property. "We're climbing into the neighbor's yard?"

He nodded, heading that way. "The deputy will take the ladder away once we're gone and keep the reporters at a distance. Sean is picking us up on the street behind yours."

Caitlyn followed him across the grass. Ian went over the fence first, then she did the same. When they reached the street, Ian's SUV was there with everyone waiting. She looked around and didn't see one reporter. She and Ian squeezed into the rear seats with Granny and Alice.

"Good thing I watch my weight," Granny murmured, "or we'd never fit in here."

Emma twisted around in the front seat and peered at Caitlyn. "I'm so glad, dear, you didn't need to answer the questions they were asking all at the same time. Even when Sean said, *No comment*, that didn't stop them."

She hoped there was a less chaotic scene at the church, but when they arrived, the reporters were held back but covered every entrance.

Sean parked, and they all poured out of the SUV. Caitlyn was the last to climb out and, as she rearranged herself beside it, she caught sight of a small mob scurrying toward them. She grasped Ian's hand.

"We knew they would be here, but they won't be inside. Keep focused on the front door," Ian whispered, following the women and Sean as though they were running interference.

It didn't work. Somehow the throng of reporters managed to separate them from the rest of their family. Ian released her hand and slung his arm around her, bringing her closer to him. Suddenly they were surrounded, and their steps were slowed to a halt.

"Why did the *Stop me!* killer blame you for the women's deaths?" one man asked, shoving a microphone into her face.

Another on her left crowded close. "Why is he targeting your patients?"

More microphones were thrust at her, and the press jostled her as they hemmed her in.

TWELVE

The killer could be in this crowd. Scanning the mob, looking for Greg especially, Ian pushed Caitlyn behind him and glared at the reporters. "No comment." Then he inched forward, slowly at first with Caitlyn following in his footsteps, but finally the press gave them some space. He was glad he'd worn his Texas Ranger star on his shirt.

When he could, he brought her around to his side, and again he slung his arm over her shoulders and sheltered her against him. The crush of reporters progressed with them until they came to the barrier the police had set up to keep the press back. Chief Franklin came toward them as several officers prevented the media from getting any closer.

The police chief walked with them toward the Longhorn Christian Church. "All I've been doing today is fielding questions instead of trying to find the killer. They started arriving in force early this morning, and then, after the radio show, Caitlyn, it seems like the numbers have doubled. I should have figured this. We have a prominent rancher and state senator and a radio talk show host involved in a serial-killer case."

"Later we need to use this to our advantage by asking for help finding Greg Quinn and his missing car." Ian glanced at Caitlyn, who had finally relaxed against him.

"And Missy," she added. "Both their photos need to be plastered everywhere."

Behind Ian, the reporters continued to shout their questions. "Let's get inside."

"I need to figure out what to say to them. Then maybe they'll leave me alone. But first I need to talk with the Shephards."

"After Jack saw the mob here at the church, he asked for Caitlyn to join him and Ruth before the funeral," Chief Franklin said.

"Good. Where are they?" Caitlyn said as they entered the church lobby.

"A conference room off the pastor's office." Chief Franklin walked to a corridor to the left. "He wants to figure out how best to handle the media with so many in town."

"How is he?" Caitlyn asked, nearing the room.

"Ruth is handling this better than Jack." The police chief took his cowboy hat off and wiped his forehead with a handkerchief.

Ian passed a room halfway down the hall that had a sign on the door for the Shephard family. "Are we meeting with only Jack and Ruth?"

"Yes. The governor is with their relatives right now." Chief Franklin knocked, then opened the door. "Caitlyn and Ian are here."

Jack stood and shook Ian's hand. "I hear there's a suspect in Jane's murder. How confident are you it's Greg Quinn?"

"There are a lot of questions surrounding him, but

we're also looking at all the possibilities in case the killer isn't Quinn. At this time, we've ruled out Clark Williams." Ian took a seat next to Caitlyn on a love seat near the Shephards.

"Don said there was another note left Saturday night." Jack gripped his wife's hand next to him.

"There are several indications that Williams isn't the murderer. One of them is he was in jail when the note was left taped to a life-size plastic doll." Ian felt Caitlyn's tension heighten at the mention of the doll.

Ruth swung her gaze to Caitlyn. "Why would Greg Quinn kill Jane? She didn't know him. For that matter, I doubt she knew Clark Williams either."

"I don't know that or why he's calling me and leaving me notes everywhere. Until the police find Greg, we won't know if he was involved."

Anger mottling his face, Jack turned to the police chief. "Why else would he be gone? What are you doing to apprehend him?"

"We'll be interviewing everyone he worked with, as well as anyone here in Longhorn who had anything to do with the Quinns. An alert has been put out for both Missy and Greg."

"Senator, we're doing everything we can. For some reason, he's still focusing on Caitlyn, even though she has protection. If he comes near her, we'll be there to nab him." That was the only choice for Ian. Circumstances interfered years ago with Caitlyn and him being together. He wanted a chance this time. Were they ever going to be together?

Ruth checked her watch. "Jack, we need to be with our families. The funeral starts soon. And remember, the governor has come from Austin."

"And we need to find a seat. I think the whole town has come out," Caitlyn said.

With tears in her eyes, Ruth approached Caitlyn and hugged her. "I appreciate you working with Jane. You helped her."

Ian had rarely seen Caitlyn speechless. Tears ran down her face, and she swallowed hard. When the Shephards left the conference room, the police chief followed to make sure everything went smoothly at the funeral.

Ian paused in front of Caitlyn with a box of tissues. "Are you ready?"

She pulled out several tissues and used one to swipe away the wet tracks on her cheeks. "Honestly—no, especially after Kelli's funeral yesterday. I can't stop thinking I'm responsible, and yet I don't know how I am."

"What the killer is doing is on him, not you. You didn't murder these women. He did."

"I know that in here." She tapped her temple. "But in here, I feel like I've done something wrong to cause this." She laid her hand over her heart.

"Then he'll have won. Don't let him. God is with you."

"Let's go. I'm glad Jack prohibited the press. This is a time we need to mourn without cameras recording every moment."

With hands joined, Ian and Caitlyn walked down the corridor to the sanctuary.

Lord, protect this town. Protect Caitlyn.

Drained emotionally and physically, Caitlyn stood at the end of the funeral service and followed Granny from the pew with Ian right behind her. His presence helped her to deal with the grief and guilt. Had she done something to cause these deaths? Why was Kelli killed first but not found until after Jane? What connected these murders? She needed to delve into the three victims' files again—and again until she figured it out. Something she was missing nagged her, but she would stay up all night if necessary to figure out what it was.

At the back of the church's nave, Caitlyn lined up to offer her condolences to the Shephard family. She turned to Ian and whispered, "I feel like I know why Jane was a victim. It's been a couple of days since I went through her folder. When we get back to the house, I want to look at it, then have you look too."

Ian lowered his head close to her ear. "Right now, don't think about the case. Deal with your grief. I'll help you any way you want later tonight. But I've had killers go on a spree where there wasn't anything that tied the victims together. It happens."

When she reached Jack and then Ruth, she hugged each one. "If I can help in any way, please let me know."

Ruth clasped Caitlyn's hand to keep her from turning away and stepped away from the crowd. "I know you think you had something to do with this, but I don't. You don't control what others do. You can only control your actions and thoughts. I hope you and the others with you will come to the ranch after this. We decided to have a party to celebrate Jane's life."

One part of her wanted to go back and comb through the three files, but the other part knew the party meant a lot to the Shephard family, and she could see Jane totally agreeing to it. She wouldn't want the sadness.

"It won't be an open house, and we certainly won't let any reporters into the party."

"I'd love to come, Ruth."

"Good because I already asked your grandmother, Emma and Alice."

Caitlyn glanced at them waiting for her and Ian. "How about Sean?"

"It's time my husband and Sean forget the past. Jane would want that. I knew she was dating someone she really liked and figured she would tell me who when she was ready. I'm so glad Sean brought her some happiness before she was killed. She may never have told you the main reason she came to see you was she'd been so upset when Marcus Browning committed suicide. They were friends, and she'd been trying to help him."

"She'd told me a friend had died but she never mentioned who."

"They went to college together."

Jack cleared his throat. "We have others waiting, Ruth."

"We'll talk later, Caitlyn. I'll see you at the ranch."

As Caitlyn joined her grandmother, she wondered if Jane knew about the young man's abuse as a child. Marcus hadn't freely talked with her when he first came to see her, but slowly he'd been opening up. That was why she'd been surprised that he killed himself.

Sean came back from looking outside. "The press is still there."

"I guess we'll have to run the gauntlet again," Emma said.

"Why don't you take the ladies first, Sean, then Caitlyn and I will leave the church? They hopefully won't bother you too much."

As most of the people at the funeral filed out, Caitlyn stood at a window near the front double doors with Ian, while Granny and the others pushed their way through the crowd of reporters. A couple of them asked questions, but Sean escorted the ladies safely to the SUV.

"Ruth wants all of us, including Sean, to come to the ranch for a get-together to celebrate Jane's life," Caitlyn said to Ian.

"I know. Jack asked me while you and Ruth were talking. All the family and close friends of theirs and Jane's have been invited. I'm surprised about Sean. Jack didn't say anything about him."

"That was Ruth's idea, and I think it would be good for Sean and Jack to put an end to this feud."

"Does Sean know?"

"Probably not. I'll tell him in the car. If he doesn't want to, that's fine, but I need to go. I found out from Ruth a piece of information I hadn't known about Jane. There may be more. Then, when we come back home, I'll go through her file."

"What did she tell you?"

Caitlyn told him as they made their way to the exit. "I'm surprised we hadn't talked about Marcus's suicide. We discussed a lot of things, but Jane never said a word about him. Ready?"

Ian nodded.

Together they left the church. As before, Ian sheltered her from the reporters, although that didn't stop some of them from gathering around the SUV and shouting the same questions as before. Sean honked his horn and eased the car forward. Finally, the press in front moved back, and Sean drove the SUV from the parking lot.

When Caitlyn told the others about the invitation to

the Shephard ranch, everyone agreed except Sean. He remained quiet. "Sean, Ruth especially wanted you to come. Jack might not have known about you and Jane, but she knew her daughter was seeing someone. You were important to Jane. That's why Ruth wants you there."

"Think about what Jane would want, dear," Emma said from the front seat. "Please. It will help you to talk about her."

Sean slanted a look at his grandmother. "I will, but I'm stopping at our ranch and getting my truck. That way, I can leave if things don't work out but y'all can stay."

At the Pierce ranch, Emma declared she would ride with Sean. Caitlyn moved to the front passenger seat, while Ian pointed the SUV toward the highway. When they approached the Shephards' gates, about ten people were prowling around until they saw Ian's car. He pulled up to a speaker and rolled down his window to announce himself and gain entry.

Immediately, an older man shoved a microphone into Ian's face. "What is the status of the case?"

"Go home. There won't be an announcement until tomorrow morning at nine at the Longhorn Police Department. You'll get all the information we can release, and the senator has agreed to make a statement then, if the media will let his family mourn Jane's death in peace today."

This was the first Caitlyn had heard about the press conference. She hoped it would keep the reporters away for the rest of the day, at least for the Shephard family.

The man conversed with the other people hanging around the gate. Slowly, several of them ambled to their vehicles and began leaving. In the meantime, Ian notified the main house he had arrived.

"Did you and Jack decide to do that?"

"Chief Franklin came up with it today and told me after the funeral. At least for a few hours, it'll give the family some breathing room."

"But there really isn't any new information."

"No, but later we're going to work. The BOLO is out on Greg Quinn throughout the country. He might be apprehended between now and then. Jack made a statement at the beginning, and he will again with some additional information about a fund being set up for any tips on the whereabouts of Quinn."

"I'm praying there is," Granny said from the back seat.

"Me too," Alice chimed in.

When the gates opened, Ian drove through, keeping an eye on the area behind his SUV in case a reporter tried to sneak in. The last media car turned around and headed in the direction of Longhorn. Before the gates closed, Sean's vehicle appeared and followed his onto the property.

There were at least thirty vehicles parked out front of the Shephards' home. They seemed to be the last of the guests to arrive, since they had left the church after most of the mourners, including Jack and Ruth. She'd hoped the press would leave once the Shephards did. But the reporters were like cattle trying to munch on the grass on the other side of the pasture fence.

One of Jane's cousins let them into the house. "I'm Patricia. The others are in the great room at the back of the house. Let me show you there."

Caitlyn didn't tell her she'd been in the Shephards'

house before and was familiar with its layout. Instead she let Jane's relative lead the way. The first person she saw in the large room that flowed out onto the deck was Sheriff Mason. He disengaged from a group he was speaking to and approached her. Emma, Granny and Alice headed for several ladies they knew, while Sean stayed with Caitlyn and Ian.

The sheriff planted himself between Ian and her. "How are you holding up, Caitlyn?"

"I'll never complain about it being quiet in Longhorn again."

Tom chuckled. "That's the way I like it too." He shifted his attention to Ian. "I just got a text that Greg Quinn's car has been discovered in a lake near Austin."

"But no Greg?" Caitlyn asked before Ian had a chance.

"No. The police are working to bring it up out of the water. We'll know more later."

"Let's hope this will lead us to the killer." Ian gestured toward the police chief coming into the room. "Does he know?"

"Yes. Since Quinn dumped his car, we're checking stolen cars reported the last few days and visiting dealerships to see if he bought something else to drive."

Chief Franklin joined them. "Tom has told you about the lead, I take it? I'm optimistic about this. If he's fled the area that means the people of Longhorn are safe."

If he's fled. She was missing something—just out of reach for her. She'd also review Missy's file. She didn't talk a lot about her husband, but Caitlyn had felt something was off there. "Excuse me. I'll leave you to talk about the case." She turned and stepped away.

When Ian stopped her, he stood close. "Are you all right?"

"I guess I won't believe it's over until he's actually caught, not just on the run. He could come back here at any time. Or he ditched his car there to focus the search in Austin rather than here."

"Do you want to go back to Nana's?"

"No, I still need to speak to Ruth again, and I want to be here for support." She scanned the guests and found Jane's mom talking with Sean. She hoped Ruth could mend the rift between the two ranch families for the Shephards' sake but for Sean's also. "We should stay for a while at least. I'm going to freshen up. I won't be long."

In the hall, Caitlyn approached a maid and asked, "Where's the powder room?"

"There are two." The young woman gave her directions to them.

When Caitlyn tried the door of the nearest one off the foyer, it was locked. Jane's cousin greeted a group of six with the mayor at the door. As Caitlyn headed for the other powder room, she realized what she really needed was some quiet and solitude after days of being in a house with five others. She was used to being alone. She ducked into the nearest vacant room, a library. Faint voices drifted to her, but at least it was much quieter in here.

She sat in a wingback, facing a wall of books. She needed to decide what other questions she would ask Ruth about Jane. As she put her purse on the floor against the leg of the chair, she flashed back to the guests in the foyer.

Rob Owens had been in the rear of the mayor's group.

She hadn't realized he was friends with the mayor. Had he known Jane well? She remembered several times she'd seen them talking at the medical clinic when Jane came for her appointments. Rob was an excellent nurse and always friendly to the patients and staff, but his appearance at the Shephards' house seemed—

She suddenly realized what had been nagging her, but how did that help the case?

She began to rise when a hand clamped on her shoulder and shoved her back down. She kicked the air, one shoe flying off. A white cloth covered her nose and mouth, and a sickly sweet smell assailed her senses.

Darkness swamped her.

THIRTEEN

While Ian waited for Caitlyn to return to the great room, he observed the various guests at the Shephards' house. The most promising sight was Sean and Ruth talking together. There was no hostility on his brother's face, and Ruth even smiled at Sean when red colored his cheeks. He'd rarely seen his brother blush.

Ian glanced at his watch. Caitlyn should have returned to the party—no, gathering in honor of Jane—by now. When she'd felt overwhelmed in the past, she would seek out a place to be alone, and he could certainly understand her feeling that way with what had happened in the past five days. The time had crawled by.

Tom read something on his phone, looked up at Ian and hurried his way. "I got a text about Greg's car. They found his body in the trunk, like Kelli."

The words and their implication slowly sank into Ian's brain. "He isn't the killer." The news paralyzed him for a few seconds before he swung around and strode toward the exit.

Where was Caitlyn? Who was the killer, then, if not Quinn or Williams?

"I need to find Caitlyn. She went to the restroom," Ian said to the sheriff, who followed him.

A maid hovered in the doorway. A guest talking to the young woman left as Ian and Tom approached.

"Where is the guest bathroom?" Ian looked up and down the corridor.

The maid gave them directions.

"You take the one near the foyer. I'll check the other by the kitchen." While Ian walked down the hallway, he glanced into all the rooms with open doors. His stomach churned like a boiling pit of acid.

When Ian found the other restroom, he knocked on the door. A deep male voice said, "I'm almost through."

A *long* minute later, the mayor emerged from the small room.

"Have you seen Caitlyn recently? I'm looking for her."

The balding man shook his head, then started down the hall but stopped after a few feet and glanced back. "I did see her a while back, when I first arrived at the house."

"How long ago?"

"Ten minutes or so."

"Was she alone?"

"Yes. If I see her, I'll let her know you're looking for her."

Ian returned to the great room and scanned it for Caitlyn. He still didn't see her, but he spied Chief Franklin and motioned for him to join him in the hallway. Moving away from the doorway, Ian texted Tom to join them. They needed to coordinate a plan to find Caitlyn. He didn't have a good feeling about this, and he never ignored his instincts.

"What's wrong?" the police chief asked.

"Caitlyn's missing." Ian explained what she was going to do and where he'd checked.

Tom approached. "I couldn't find her."

"We now know Greg isn't the killer. It's possible Caitlyn was taken by the real one. We need to search the whole house." Ian's heartbeat increased at a dizzying pace at the thought of Caitlyn being the next victim—the question mark on the note left Saturday night. "Don, can you let Jack know what we're doing and keep all the guests in the great room, while Tom and I go through the ground floor first? No one should leave."

"Will do." The police chief hurried down the corridor.

"Call for backup. I don't have a good feeling about this, Tom."

The sheriff nodded. "I'll cover this side of the house while you go through the left part. A couple of deputies will be here soon if we have to expand our search to the second and third floors."

As Ian passed the great room, Chief Franklin was talking to Jack. The senator's face paled. Ian accelerated his pace, praying he was overreacting to the situation. He first went through the den, opening and closing any door he encountered. Nothing. He moved to the next room, an office. He checked behind furniture and anyplace where Caitlyn could be.

What if he found her dead like the other victims?

Lord, help me find her—alive!

For years he'd turned away from God, but in the past few he'd realized that, instead of distancing himself from the Lord, he'd needed more than anything to grow closer. Strengthening his relationship with Him had made his job less stressful—knowing He was always there.

Now I need You more than ever. I love Caitlyn. I don't want to lose her.

When he entered the library, his gaze zoomed in on Caitlyn's purse on the floor by a chair. He rushed around to see if she'd been concealed from his view by the high-back somehow. She wasn't there.

He swept around to figure out if she could be somewhere else in the room. Again he investigated everywhere she could be hidden from view. She wasn't in here, but she wouldn't have left without her purse. Ian returned to the chair and scoured the area around it for clues.

That was when he spied one of her flat black shoes mostly concealed under the skirt of the couch.

Caitlyn had been taken.

Slowly, the fog cleared from Caitlyn's mind, but she remained still, lying on some kind of mattress, a musky odor replacing the smell she remembered right before she'd passed out. Was it chloroform? Her head throbbed against her skull. The bite of the twine on her wrists and ankles told her she was tied up. She listened for any sound to indicate a person was nearby. Nothing. The eerie silence underscored how alone she was.

Was this how Jane, Kelli and Missy had been taken?

She remembered seeing Rob Owens right before she went into the library. Was he involved? She would never have suspected him. He'd always been friendly and helpful to anyone at the clinic. She had a hard time seeing Rob as the killer. Was there someone else at the Shephards' house who was the killer?

Maybe she was wrong.

What if Clark Williams had been released on bail today and he'd come after her? It had seemed unlikely he was the killer. Clark still had a grudge against her because Kelli finally left him, and he blamed her for that. This might have nothing to do with the other murders. If that were the case, she had a chance of talking him out of doing any bodily harm to her.

The creaking of a door alerted her she wasn't alone anymore.

The sound of footsteps approaching the bed sent alarm through her body. Her muscles stiffened, preparing her to take a strike. With her breath bottled in her lungs, she waited.

"Quit playing games. I know you're awake."

The female voice froze Caitlyn to her core.

Ian met the sheriff and police chief in the foyer. "No sign of Caitlyn. Have the other searchers checked in?"

Tom nodded. "Nothing was caught on their security cameras. Whoever took Caitlyn knew where the cameras were and avoided them. Except for one at the front gates. There were three cars that left the ranch within the time frame of when she was kidnapped. Two were employees', and the other was a stolen vehicle, taken near Austin yesterday."

"We need to focus on the stolen car. I also have an officer going to each employee's home to talk with them. Maybe they saw something. One didn't exit too long after the stolen car went through the front gates."

Ian's mind churned with all the possibilities of what could go wrong. "Then it's feasible the kidnapper killed Greg Quinn, stole the car and drove here to take Caitlyn. When did the stolen car come to the ranch? With the funeral attendees?" He tamped down any thoughts except ones centered on this case.

"I'll see that the camera is checked for when the car came to the ranch." Chief Franklin's cell phone rang. "Excuse me."

The sheriff's frown deepened. "I know it might be too late, but we're working with the highway patrol officers to have roadblocks set up on all the roads out of here. If the kidnapper is in the area, we'll get him."

But was it too late for Caitlyn? "Did the security photo of the stolen car show the person driving? If he lives here, he could hole up somewhere and wait us out. How about traffic cams? Anything on them?"

"The windows in the car were tinted, and the photo didn't capture the driver's face. There was no stolen car on the traffic cams around the time of the kidnapping, but we don't have many in place. Most are around the town. There are a lot of places to hide outside of Longhorn."

"And there's always the possibility he left here and is far away from the ranch by now."

"An alert has been issued statewide and for the surrounding states. We're using the press in town to spread the word. It's gone national."

The sound of a helicopter flying overhead reinforced the extent of help with the kidnapping. "I hope he's still driving the stolen car, but this person has been one step ahead of us and bold. He most likely has another vehicle stashed somewhere else and has already traded it."

Chief Franklin joined them, sliding his phone into his pocket. "The stolen car was found not far from here on this side of the lake. The helicopter spotted it from the air. They didn't see anyone around it, but their view was hampered by the tree cover."

"Tom and I will go investigate it, while you deal with the guests. See who was attending the party but isn't here now."

"Don't worry about here. Just find Caitlyn." The police chief gave Ian and Tom the location. "I'll finish up speaking with the last few guests while my officers interview the senator's staff. I'll let you know if we find out any useful information. Maybe someone saw something and doesn't know its significance."

"I hope so." Ian started for the front door. "I'm driving." He had to do something or he'd go crazy with worry. He'd seen the work of the killer when he was through with his victims. He had to save Caitlyn from that fate. He had to keep going, remain focused.

Ian sped away from the house, only slowing for the gate to open. When he took the turn onto the road around the lake, the rear of his car fishtailed. He steered his SUV straight and kept going.

"I'd like to reach the stolen vehicle in one piece." Tom gripped the edge of the seat.

"She's already been gone for a couple of hours. You know how important time is in cases like this." He'd let her down. He should have been able to protect her.

When Ian pulled up to the brown sedan, he snapped on his latex gloves and jumped out of the car before Tom. He had to know if she was in the trunk like Kelli had been. His heartbeat hammered against his rib cage. Tom said something, but all Ian heard was the thundering of his pulse in his ears.

His hand shook as he punched the trunk button by the driver's seat. The *pop* of it opening shuddered through him as he made his way to the rear. When he stepped around to look inside, he closed his eyes after the sight of the empty trunk.

Thank You, Lord. I still have a chance to rescue her.

His gaze lit upon Caitlyn's other black flat. It taunted Ian. Was it left accidentally or on purpose? "She was in here." He lifted the shoe and dropped it in an evidence bag Tom held out. "Before we start processing the car, let's check the area. Did they walk or drive away?"

Ian took the left half while Tom worked the right side. Immediately around the vehicle, there were no obvious signs of tire tracks other than the stolen sedan's. "Let's expand our search. I wish the ground wasn't so hard and dry. Even footprints would help tell which direction he went with Caitlyn. Are there any cabins around here?"

"A couple on this side. I'm calling one of my deputies to come and search the car for any further evidence while we investigate them." Tom took out his cell phone.

"Good. How about using a boat? What if the kidnapper had a small craft waiting here to throw us off?" This part of the lake had only one way in or out, but once on open water, there would be a lot of places he could take Caitlyn.

"I'll have the helicopter fly over the lake and report anything suspicious."

Ian used the time to walk to the edge of the lake and scour the brush and rocky surface for any signs of a boat having been there. Had Caitlyn left the shoe in the trunk on purpose? If so, then was there some other sign she'd left them to follow? She was a fighter and wouldn't go down without a battle—unless she was knocked out or dead.

He pivoted to go back to his SUV. Out of the corner of his eye, he caught sight of a boot print in the muddy edge of the lake near the stony shoreline. Another one was partly in the water and was losing its definition. Ian quickly took pictures of what he found. The person who'd planted them and was possibly Caitlyn's kidnapper wore either a size eleven or twelve shoe.

"Tom, I found boot prints. We need a boat patrol."

The sheriff closed the distance between them. "I agree. I couldn't find any tire tracks except the ones the sedan made."

Ian's cell phone rang, and he quickly answered the call from Chief Franklin. "Any leads?"

"More information than a lead. The stolen car came into the ranch when the caterers entered. The lady that owns the catering company said there was a brown car behind them. She didn't think much of it. There was a lot of activity at that time, with some of the staff getting ready for the guests during the funeral. Again the driver of the vehicle wasn't caught on the camera."

"Thanks. We think the kidnapper used a boat to get away after ditching the brown sedan."

"That's a good-sized lake with a lot of coves. I'll let you know if I discover anything else to help you find Caitlyn."

"How is Sally holding up?"

"She's a tough lady. She's sure you're going to find the kidnapper in time. Sean and Emma are staying by her side."

When Ian disconnected the call, he faced the lake, his gaze skimming the shoreline.

Lord, I can't do this without You. I found Caitlyn again, and I can't lose her this time.

Caitlyn opened her eyes, the bright overhead light blinding her for a few seconds until Missy Quinn hovered over her. Why hadn't Caitlyn seen the resemblance before today?

"You're related to Marcus Browning." Caitlyn saw it in the eyes and the chin line. Marcus had had blond hair like Missy but a darker shade. She was petite but not frail-looking as Marcus had been.

"He's my twin. He came to you for help and instead he ended up killing himself. You were supposed to save him." The hatred in her expression and words blasted Caitlyn.

And, for a few seconds, she felt she deserved the blame for Marcus's suicide. "I tried to help him. He was making progress. I was shocked when I found him dead."

"I'm sure that lets you sleep at night. But it's a lie. Now you're going to pay for that just as soon as my brother comes back."

"Brother?"

"Yes. You know him as Rob Owens. He had a great time destroying your office."

"His name isn't Rob Owens?"

"No. He's my younger brother and he has always done what I ask. He loved Marcus and was devastated when he died."

Caitlyn's head pounded from the chloroform she'd been forced to breathe. She shoved the pain from her mind. If she could delay their plans, she might have a chance to get loose, or Ian might find her.

"His credentials were falsified. It helped he had criminal connections," Missy said.

"He was good at his job, from what I heard."

"He was an orderly for two years." Missy checked the ropes around Caitlyn's ankles to make sure they were secure, then rolled her onto her side to inspect her hands bound behind her back. "I'm proud of my younger brother. He went in and out of your office at will. You had no idea he took your extra set of keys and made copies for me, but it sure helped. I didn't even have to break into your house, but I did just to throw the police off." She turned away.

"Why kill Jane, Kelli and your husband?"

Missy stiffened and balled her hands. When she twisted back toward her, deep lines on her face portrayed the depth of her anger. "Marcus was in love with Jane, and she wouldn't have him."

"They were friends."

"Is that what she said? She lied. He cried on the phone to me about her, not long before he killed himself. I couldn't let her live when he didn't. Or you."

"Then why did you murder Kelli and Greg?"

"I needed someone to throw off the police. Kelli was easy to get to and fit the bill as one of your patients. Greg hadn't been planned. He came in when I was setting up the crime scene in my house. I knocked him out and, when Lex came to help me do something with Greg, we decided to make it look like he was the murderer. My brother killed him."

"He was your husband!"

Missy strode toward the exit and glanced back with a smile of hatred on her face. "I'm gonna miss him, but at least you'll pay for Marcus's suicide. I wanted you to suffer longer, but I had to settle for at least calling you out on national radio. I enjoyed seeing the reporters going after you." She opened the door and flipped off the overhead light. "Lex will be back soon, so cherish your last moments alive." Her cackles trailed her from the room.

The second Missy left, Caitlyn struggled to sit up on the bed and stared at her feet. She tried to bend over far enough to reach the rope around her ankles. She couldn't. Breathing hard, she lay back down on the covered mattress that smelled putrid—like dried... blood. Bile rose in her throat, but she choked it back. She couldn't think about what else had happened on this mattress. She had to free herself and get the police.

When she tried to yank her hands apart to loosen the twine, it cut into her wrists. She stared up at the ceiling in the darkened room, trying to come up with a way to rid herself of her shackles. After rolling onto her front, she contorted her body until her behind was in the air, her cheek pressed into the covers. If she could wiggle her bound wrists over her bottom, she might be able to bring them in front of her. She had two things going for her: her long arms and determination.

Missy and Rob would not get away with this.

She pushed herself up to a kneeling position. Sweat ran in rivulets down her face. With her wrists parted slightly, the rope digging into her flesh, she twisted and squirmed until she brought her hands down the back of her legs. She yanked her ankles apart, giving her some flexibility to finish bringing her arms around to the front.

Exhausted, she sat for a moment trying to get enough strength to work on loosening her bindings to free herself. She raised her bound hands to her face and used her teeth to work on the knots. If she had to chew through the thick string, she would.

They were not going to win.

The chafing of the twine rubbed into her wrists, making a bloody mess. She kept at it. This might be her only chance.

When the minutes ticked into half an hour, she finally slackened a knot enough to release her hands. Next, she attacked the bindings around her ankles to free her legs. Soon, she scrambled off the bed, taking the covers with her in her haste. The door was locked. She'd heard it click into place when Missy left. When the overhead light had been on, she'd noticed a window in the middle of the wall to her right.

As she felt her way in that direction, she could make out faint objects in the room as her eyes had grown accustomed to the dark. When she reached the side, she moved to the left with her hand patting the wall for the window above her. She touched the bottom of it, gripped the curtains and slid them open.

In the light, she glimpsed a chair not far away that she could use to stand on. She retrieved it and stood on it to hoist herself up and out the small window. She felt around until she found the lock and released it. Then she gripped the sill and labored to pull herself up.

She could see now that she was in a cabin surrounded by woods. The noise of a car pulling up to it spurred her to move faster. She prayed it was the police, but if it wasn't, she needed to be away from here when Rob returned. Hanging halfway out of the window, she estimated the distance to the ground was a ten-foot drop. She had no choice. The only way out was to plunge headfirst, since the opening was too small for her to wiggle herself around to go feetfirst.

The sound of voices drifted to her. Not the police. Rob and Missy. Defeat taunted her.

No!

She dived toward the ground, trying to protect her head by tucking herself into a ball. Her right shoulder took the brunt of the fall. Pain streaked through her, a groan escaping from her.

Ian stood in a boat with Tom, both of them searching the shore with binoculars. The sun would be going down in an hour. Although they had infrared capability if needed, searching in the dark would make the situation twice as difficult. He had to find Caitlyn before that.

When his cell phone rang, he quickly answered the call from the police chief. "Please have good news. We've checked what cabins we've seen from the boat, but nothing so far."

"When I interviewed the mayor, we discovered one of the people at the reception had not been invited, and there's a link to Caitlyn and the medical clinic. Rob Owens. I sent officers to the clinic and his apartment. I've put a BOLO out on his car too."

Ian remembered the male nurse who had helped them take the boxes to the SUV a few days before. "You think he's the killer?"

"A very promising person of interest. Why did he come to the party uninvited unless he had an ulterior motive?"

"Keep me informed. Check into the possibility he owns a cabin at the lake."

Sliding his phone into his pocket, Ian let Tom know about the development.

"He worked with Caitlyn?"

"Not with her but at the same clinic."

"There's a connection between the killer and the ladies murdered if Rob Owens is the person we're looking for."

Ian and Tom went back to searching the shoreline as the sun set and bright colors splashed across the western horizon.

Was Owens holed up somewhere at the lake or in his car miles away from Longhorn? Was time running out?

As dusk fell, Chief Franklin called again. "We located the area of the lake he's driving toward on a traffic cam. He has a red sports car." He gave Ian the license number and directions.

Ian informed the deputy driving the boat, who altered their course while Tom informed the other law enforcement officers searching. Using his binoculars again, Ian scoured the shoreline. As they neared the area where Owens might be, through the trees Ian spied a red car. He must have just arrived.

Two people ran out of the cabin toward the left side—not to the car. Shadows obscured his view of them.

Ian pointed in the direction of the cabin. "I think that's Owens and another person, possibly Caitlyn, but it could be someone else."

While Ian kept his attention on the pair, the pilot swung the boat and headed for the shoreline as fast as he could in the growing dark. Through the lenses, Ian followed the couple plunging into the forest.

When the boat neared the shore, Ian and Tom readied themselves with their weapons and infrared goggles for later when it would be too dark to see well. They jumped into a foot of water and hurried to dry ground.

"Inform the rest of the searchers. We need backup," Tom said to the deputy manning the boat.

"Check inside." Ian ran toward the left side of the

cabin. He didn't want to lose the two people. One had to be Owens since the red sports car with the correct license plate number was parked in front.

He slowed his pace when he caught sight of the open window. He inspected the ground. It appeared someone might have had a scuffle here or—he looked up—fell out of the window.

Tom came around the corner. "No one is inside, but someone was tied up. There's blood on the bindings. I also found blood on a mattress. This might be the place where they killed Kelli and Jane."

Blood. He prayed Caitlyn was still alive and might have escaped. Ian gestured toward where he saw the couple go into the woods. "They went that way."

Did Caitlyn climb out of the window? Was the second person with Owens Caitlyn or someone else? As the forest enveloped Ian in dark shadows, he prayed Caitlyn was alive when he found the pair. Soon they would have to put on the infrared goggles, which he hoped would give him and Tom an advantage.

The sound of a gunshot reverberated through the woods. Ian sped in the direction of the noise, his gaze sweeping the terrain.

When a bullet struck a tree trunk nearby, Caitlyn zigzagged away from it and dived into the brush, hoping the wall of greenery and the dimness would give her some cover to get away. She crawled deeper into the bushes and thick ground cover. While the approach of night could help her, it could also hinder her. She had no idea where she was going.

The pounding of footsteps grew closer. She kept

moving away, her heart pounding even louder and faster.

She ran into an impregnable barrier of green. Darkness completely enveloped her. Would it protect her from her pursuers? She could hear the snap of twigs and their heavy breathing as Rob and Missy drew nearer.

Trapped. Nowhere to go. Did Ian know what was going on?

FOURTEEN

With Tom behind him, Ian raced through the woods as fast as he could without making a sound, searching for any sign of someone's presence. As it grew murkier, he put on his goggles while moving forward. No time to waste. When he glimpsed two heat signatures about thirty yards ahead, both stationary, he slowed.

The man lifted a gun and shot several rounds into the thick brush in front of him. When the woman did the same, Ian was sure it wasn't Caitlyn. He signaled for the sheriff to move to the right while he went left. If they could sneak up on the pair, they could catch them unawares.

His attention glued to the couple, he crept closer until he was only a few yards away and could hear them whispering but not what they were saying. From behind and with the infrared aid, he couldn't tell who the woman was, although he was sure it wasn't Caitlyn. His goal was to subdue the two of them, then search for her. He wouldn't rest until he found her.

As Ian progressed toward the couple, Tom did too. Several feet away, with the pair's focus on the thicket in front of them, Ian paused and lifted his weapon at Owens, while Tom covered the female.

Ian stuffed down the rage at what these two had done in Longhorn. He had to remain calm and in control. "Drop your guns, put your hands in the air and turn around slowly. Don't give me a reason to shoot you."

Owens tossed his revolver onto the ground a few feet away and swung around, his hands clenched at his sides.

"Raise your arms, Owens. And, lady, I suggest you do the same. The sheriff has his gun trained on you."

A long moment passed.

"Peggy, do as he says. It's over." Owens lifted his arms into the air.

"Step away from her," Ian said, every sense on high alert.

Owens did as he was told, putting several feet between him and the woman. With her back still to Ian and Tom, she threw her weapon into the brush, her scream of frustration and anger nerve-jangling.

Ian nodded toward the sheriff. They moved in. Looking for any sign Owens would challenge him, Ian grabbed his handcuffs with one hand while holding his gun on the suspect with the other. "Get down on the ground."

Owens complied, and Ian hurried to cuff the killer so if he needed to help Tom with the woman, he could.

"Peggy, get down and put your hands behind your back," Tom said in his deep, commanding voice.

Another long moment crawled by.

Sounds of others approaching echoed through the woods. The beams from flashlights danced about the trees, giving Ian enough illumination to take his goggles off.

The woman looked in the direction the backup was coming from and crumbled to the ground as though finally realizing she had been caught. Tom secured her, while Ian hauled Owens to his feet.

As the area brightened further with the approach of three deputies, Ian passed Owens to an officer, then walked to the edge of the brush and shone his flashlight into the dark foliage. "Caitlyn, it's Ian. We've caught Owens. You're safe! Let me know where you are, and I'll come get you." He glanced over his shoulder and saw the woman's face in good light for the first time. Surprise snatched his voice for a few seconds. "And Missy has been caught." His heartbeat thumped against his chest.

"I'm over here."

Ian swung his flashlight in the direction of Caitlyn's voice. She stood in the middle of the thick vegetation, blood dripping down her arm.

The throbbing pain where a bullet had ripped straight through the fleshy part of Caitlyn's left arm pulled her from a restless sleep. Streaks of sunlight streamed through the slits in the curtains into the bedroom at Emma's. The trauma of the previous night was over. She should be relieved and happy the killers were caught, but all she felt was sadness for all who had been touched by Lex and Peggy, the siblings of Marcus Browning.

Caitlyn stared at the ceiling. Such hatred and anger in the pair had driven them to exact revenge on her and Jane. Their actions had led to more destruction and pain. But in the end, they were caught, and they would spend the rest of their lives in jail—all because they wanted to get back at the two women. God had it right.

The only way to deal with pain and anger at someone was to forgive the person. It sounded easy, but it was hard to do without the Lord's help. She should know. She'd been carrying anger at Byron around for seventeen years. Her feelings generated by that intense rage had guided and directed her life for too long. She'd missed an opportunity to be with Ian years ago.

The door opened slowly. Granny popped her head in and looked toward the bed. "You're awake. I just needed to check on you and make sure you're all right."

Sitting up, she smiled at her grandmother. "I'll be fine. Now, where is everyone?"

"Emma is in the kitchen making another pot of coffee. Sean and Alice went back to the ranch, and Ian is at the sheriff's office, most likely dotting all his i's and crossing all his t's. He wants nothing to go wrong with his case against the killers. He called for the tenth time to ask how you were doing. He'll be here as soon as he can."

Caitlyn swung her legs off the bed. "I'm getting up. The coffee smells great. I'll be in the kitchen soon."

Granny stared at the sling holding her left arm. "Do you need any help getting dressed?"

"I'll manage. Since I'll be this way for a while, I need to figure out how to do it on my own."

"It's okay to ask for help. That's why I'm here."

"I know, Granny."

After her grandmother shut the door behind her, Caitlyn stood slowly, still weak from the loss of blood last night. At least she hadn't had to stay at the medical center after they'd patched up her arm and checked to make sure her shoulder was okay. She would be sore from her dive out the cabin window, but she would be able to use her right arm.

As she wrestled with a pair of sweatpants and a short-sleeved button-up shirt, she remembered the last time she'd seen Ian. He'd ridden in the ambulance with her, holding her hand the whole way, saying little but absorbing her presence. As a deputy waited for him at the medical center, he'd kissed her lips right before she was wheeled into the ER.

She had so much to talk to him about.

In the kitchen, Granny and Emma sat at the table, and there was a full cup of coffee before an empty seat. As Caitlyn took a long sip, the doorbell rang. Tensing, she straightened.

"You don't need to worry. The killers are locked up." Emma hurried out of the kitchen and returned a minute later holding a vase of roses. "You got flowers, Caitlyn."

From Ian? She plucked the note from the bouquet and slid the card out to read. "'Thank you for helping me. From a listener of *Share with Caitlyn.*'" She looked from Emma to Granny. "That's sweet." But she wasn't sure what she should do going forward—not after what had happened. "I don't know if I'm going to continue counseling and doing my show."

Granny harrumphed. "You can't let them win."

"But Jane, Kelli and Greg are dead because I couldn't help Marcus."

"Did you do your best?" Granny's lips thinned into a hard line.

"I thought so."

"Then you did what you could. Some people ask for help but don't really want it. If a doctor stopped practicing when he lost a patient, we wouldn't have many capable doctors to help us when we need it."

Emma set the roses on the table. "Come with me. I think you need to see something."

Caitlyn followed Emma into the dining room. Her jaw dropped at the sight on the table that could seat eight. It was covered from one end to the other with gifts from flowers to chocolate.

Emma took her hand. "And that's not all. Come into the living room." She swept her arm toward the presents sitting in every available space. "The den filled up first. They started coming early this morning. Your radio listeners believe in you, but some of these gifts are from people in town also."

When the doorbell rang again, Caitlyn said, "I'll go."

Granny walked with her to answer it and ended up taking a large chocolate-and-fruit arrangement made to look like flowers, since Caitlyn's arm was in the sling. "I'll take this. Go see the den, then come back and tell me you haven't helped anyone. That note you read in the kitchen is like all of the messages you've received."

"I'm going to fix you lunch. I'll let you know when it's ready." Emma headed back into the kitchen.

Caitlyn made her way to the den. Granny followed but stayed at the threshold. As Caitlyn moved from one gift to the next and read the notes attached, emotions soon knotted in her throat. Words escaped her at the outpouring of support and best wishes for a quick recovery. A lot from people she didn't know.

"I didn't realize." Caitlyn sank onto the couch and stared at the vibrant array of flowers and colorful gifts, at all the different ways chocolate could be used. "How did they know I love flowers and chocolate?"

"I recalled you mentioning it on-air a couple of times when replying to a question. Your listeners remember." Granny glanced to the side. "I'm going to help Emma with lunch."

Her grandmother scurried away before Caitlyn could ask her to stay. She didn't know if she wanted to be alone with the memories of the past week's events. Then Ian appeared in the doorway with a smile on his face.

He closed the distance between them and sat next to her, drawing her close to him. "I've missed you so much, but I wanted to make sure Lex and Peggy, aka Rob and Missy, aren't going anywhere but to jail. With the evidence we have, they will be in prison for life. The case is solid." He turned slightly toward her and cupped her face with one hand. "Now I can devote my time to you. We have seventeen years to make up for. Just so you know my intentions right up front, I love you, and someday I hope we'll marry. My bachelor days are behind me."

Tears blurred her vision. She covered his cradling hand with her own, turned his over and kissed his palm. "I love you. I'm not going to let anyone come between us again."

Ian leaned forward and took her mouth in a kiss that he poured all his love into, and Caitlyn matched him. In twenty-four hours, her life had completely changed.

When they finally parted their lips, he rested his forehead against hers. "I'm glad I don't have an allergy to flowers. Where did all these come from?"

She laughed. "From all over the country! A lot of them from listeners to my show. They want me back as soon as possible. I'd been considering a change in career, but I've been convinced not to."

"Good because I have a question for you. How long should a couple wait to marry after declaring their love to each other?"

She tilted her head to the side and tapped her forefinger against her chin. "Well, let me see. That'll depend on the state marriage laws."

"In Texas, it's three days."

"Then, my answer is *three days*," Caitlyn said, then drew his head toward hers and kissed him long and hard.

A year later

Ian pulled up in front of his house at the Pierce ranch, a smaller version of the one Sean lived in. After parking, he ran around and opened the rear passenger door and lifted out his two-day-old son from his baby seat.

"Michael, this is your home." He held his son up to see the redbrick, sprawling ranch-style house for a few seconds, then he cradled him in the crook of his arm while opening the door for Caitlyn. Using his free hand, he helped her from the SUV.

"I'm glad to be home. I didn't get any rest in the hospital. It'll be nice having Granny at our house for a while helping with our son."

Ian gave her a quick kiss on the mouth, then passed Michael to her. "Honey," he put his hand on the front doorknob and turned it, allowing her to go in first, "this might not be the time to get rest."

Across the foyer hung a banner welcoming Michael and Caitlyn home, and family and friends stood applauding beneath it. She looked back at Ian.

He shrugged. "Sean and Alice planned it. Oh, and I think Nana and Sally helped with the party."

Caitlyn took several more steps into the house and immediately was surrounded by the guests, all wanting a peek at Michael.

"May I hold him?" Melanie asked.

Caitlyn gave Michael to her radio-show producer, who had been dating Sean for the past several months. Ian's brother was finally getting his life together, and Melanie would be perfect for Sean. Ian hoped something good would come from them dating.

As the guests moved into the living room, Ian slipped his arm around his wife and drew her next to him. "I never thought I would be a dad, but I'm loving every minute."

Caitlyn chuckled. "Wait until you have to get up in the middle of the night to take care of him."

"Who, me?"

"Sure. We're in this together. Equal partners."

Ian paused, pulled her close and kissed her with all the love he felt for her.

* * * * *

If you loved this exciting romantic suspense,
pick up the other books in
Margaret Daley's LONE STAR JUSTICE *miniseries*

HIGH RISK REUNION
LONE STAR CHRISTMAS RESCUE

And be sure to check out
Margaret's previous miniseries
ALASKAN SEARCH AND RESCUE

THE YULETIDE RESCUE
TO SAVE HER CHILD
THE PROTECTOR'S MISSION
STANDOFF AT CHRISTMAS

Available now from Love Inspired Suspense!

Find more great reads at www.LoveInspired.com.

Dear Readers,

Texas Ranger Showdown is my third book in my Lone Star Justice series about Texas Rangers, the state police in Texas. I love writing about strong heroes and heroines. In this story, I wanted my heroine to be the target of a killer who made it personal and taunted her. As a therapist, Caitlyn had faced a traumatic situation that had changed her life. She used her pain to help others solve their problems. She had to dig deep to deal with the killer who wanted to destroy Caitlyn's life.

I love hearing from readers. You can contact me at margaretdaley@gmail.com or at PO Box 2074 Tulsa, OK 74101. You can also learn more about my books at www.margaretdaley.com. I have a monthly newsletter that you can sign up for on my website.

Best wishes,

Margaret Daley

COMING NEXT MONTH FROM
Love Inspired® Suspense

Available May 8, 2018

BOUND BY DUTY
Military K-9 Unit • by Valerie Hansen

When Sgt. Linc Colson is assigned to monitor Zoe Sullivan and determine if she's secretly aiding her fugitive serial killer brother, his instincts tell him she's not in league with the criminal—she's in danger. It's up to him and his K-9 partner, Star, to keep the pretty single mom alive.

PRIMARY SUSPECT
Callahan Confidential • by Laura Scott

Framed for the murder of his ex-girlfriend—and then attacked at the crime scene—fire investigator Mitch Callahan turns to ER nurse Dana Petrie for help. As they fight for their lives, can she be convinced of his innocence—and in his promise of love?

RODEO STANDOFF
McKade Law • by Susan Sleeman

Deputy Tessa McKade knows the rodeo is a dangerous place, but she never expected she'd come close to losing her life there. Having detective Braden Hayes act as her bodyguard is as much of a surprise as the feelings she's developing for him. Will she survive long enough to see them through?

PLAIN OUTSIDER
by Alison Stone

She thought leaving her Amish community was tough; now Deputy Becky Spoth is the target of a stalker. Her only ally is fellow deputy Harrison James. She'll rely on him to stay ahead of her pursuer, yet can she trust him not to break her heart?

DYING TO REMEMBER
by Sara K. Parker

After a gunshot wound to the head, Ella Camden turns to the only man who'll believe she's being targeted, ex-love and security expert Roman DeHart. When her attacker strikes again, Roman intensifies his bodyguard duties. He let her go once; this time he'll do whatever it takes to make sure she stays alive—and his—forever.

FUGITIVE PURSUIT
by Christa Sinclair

Schoolteacher Jamie Carter is a fugitive! But she's only hiding her niece to keep her safe from her murderous sheriff father. Bounty hunter Zack Owen goes from hunting Jamie down to protecting her and the little girl—no matter the personal price.

LOOK FOR THESE AND OTHER LOVE INSPIRED BOOKS WHEREVER BOOKS ARE SOLD, INCLUDING MOST BOOKSTORES, SUPERMARKETS, DISCOUNT STORES AND DRUGSTORES.

LISCNM0418

Get 2 Free Books,
Plus 2 Free Gifts—
just for trying the Reader Service!

YES! Please send me 2 FREE Love Inspired® Suspense novels and my 2 FREE mystery gifts (gifts are worth about $10 retail). After receiving them, if I don't wish to receive any more books, I can return the shipping statement marked "cancel." If I don't cancel, I will receive 4 brand-new novels every month and be billed just $5.24 each for the regular-print edition or $5.74 each for the larger-print edition in the U.S., or $5.74 each for the regular-print edition or $6.24 each for the larger-print edition in Canada. That's a savings of at least 13% off the cover price. It's quite a bargain! Shipping and handling is just 50¢ per book in the U.S. and 75¢ per book in Canada*. I understand that accepting the 2 free books and gifts places me under no obligation to buy anything. I can always return a shipment and cancel at any time. The free books and gifts are mine to keep no matter what I decide.

Please check one: ☐ Love Inspired Suspense Regular-Print   ☐ Love Inspired Suspense Larger-Print
                        (153/353 IDN GMWT)   (107/307 IDN GMWT)

Name	(PLEASE PRINT)	
Address		Apt. #
City	State/Prov.	Zip/Postal Code

Signature (if under 18, a parent or guardian must sign)

Mail to the **Reader Service:**
IN U.S.A.: P.O. Box 1341, Buffalo, NY 14240-8531
IN CANADA: P.O. Box 603, Fort Erie, Ontario L2A 5X3

Want to try two free books from another line?
Call 1-800-873-8635 or visit www.ReaderService.com.

* Terms and prices subject to change without notice. Prices do not include applicable taxes. Sales tax applicable in N.Y. Canadian residents will be charged applicable taxes. Offer not valid in Quebec. This offer is limited to one order per household. Books received may not be as shown. Not valid for current subscribers to Love Inspired Suspense books. All orders subject to approval. Credit or debit balances in a customer's account(s) may be offset by any other outstanding balance owed by or to the customer. Please allow 4 to 6 weeks for delivery. Offer available while quantities last.

Your Privacy—The Reader Service is committed to protecting your privacy. Our Privacy Policy is available online at www.ReaderService.com or upon request from the Reader Service.

We make a portion of our mailing list available to reputable third parties that offer products we believe may interest you. If you prefer that we not exchange your name with third parties, or if you wish to clarify or modify your communication preferences, please visit us at www.ReaderService.com/consumerchoice or write to us at Reader Service Preference Service, P.O. Box 9062, Buffalo, NY 14240-9062. Include your complete name and address.

LIS17R3

Looking for inspiration in tales
of hope, faith and heartfelt romance?

Check out **Love Inspired**® and
Love Inspired® Suspense books!

New books available every month!

CONNECT WITH US AT:

Harlequin.com/Community

 Facebook.com/HarlequinBooks

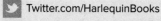 Twitter.com/HarlequinBooks

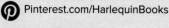 Instagram.com/HarlequinBooks

Pinterest.com/HarlequinBooks

ReaderService.com

LIGENRE2018